NOV 2 1 2017

THE STORY OF
ARTHUR
TRULUV

THE STORY OF
ARTHUR
TRULUV

A NOVEL

Elizabeth Berg

RANDOM HOUSE

NEW YORK

Published in the United States by Random House, an imprint and division of Penguin Random House LLC, New York.

RANDOM HOUSE and the HOUSE colophon are registered trademarks of Penguin Random House LLC.

Library of Congress Cataloging-in-Publication Data
Names: Berg, Elizabeth, author.
Title: The Story of Arthur Truluv : a novel / Elizabeth Berg.
Description: New York : Random House, [2017]
Identifiers: LCCN 2016047564| ISBN 9781400069903 (hardcover : acid-free paper) | ISBN 9780679605133 (ebook)
Subjects: LCSH: Interpersonal relations—Fiction. | Teenage girls—Fiction. | Widowers—Fiction. | BISAC: FICTION / Contemporary Women. | FICTION / Family Life. | FICTION / Literary.
Classification: LCC PS3552.E6996 S76 2017 | DDC 813/.54—dc23
LC record available at https://lccn.loc.gov/2016047564

Printed in the United States of America on acid-free paper

randomhousebooks.com

9 8 7 6 5 4 3 2 1

First Edition

Book design by Jo Anne Metsch

For my daughters,
Julie Krintzman and Jennifer Berta

We all know that *something* is eternal. And it ain't houses and it ain't names, and it ain't earth, and it ain't even the stars—everybody knows in their bones that *something* is eternal, and that something has to do with human beings.

—THORNTON WILDER, *Our Town*

Act well your part, there all the honour lies.

—ALEXANDER POPE, "An Essay on Man"

THE STORY OF
ARTHUR
TRULUV

I n the six months since the November day that his wife, Nola, was buried, Arthur Moses has been having lunch with her every day. He rides the bus to the cemetery and when he gets there, he takes his sweet time walking over to her plot: she will be there no matter when he arrives. She will be there and be there and be there.

Today he lingers near the headstone of Adelaide Marsh, two rows over from Nola, ten markers down. Adelaide was born April 3, 1897, died November 18, 1929. Arthur does the math, slowly. Thirty-two. Then he calculates again, because he thinks it would be wrong to stand near someone's grave thinking about how old they were the day they died and be off by a year. Or more. Math has always been difficult for Arthur, even on paper; he describes himself as numerically illiterate. Nola did the checkbook, but now he does. He tries, anyway; he gets out his giant-size calculator and pays a great deal of attention to what he's doing, he doesn't even keep the radio on, but more often than not he ends up with astronomically improbable sums. Sometimes he goes to the bank and they help him, but it's an embarrassment and an inconvenience. "We all have our gifts," Nola used to say, and she was right. Arthur's gift is working the land; he was a groundskeeper for the parks before he retired many years ago. He still keeps a nice rose garden in the front of his house; the vegetable garden in the back he has let go.

But yes, thirty-two is how old Adelaide Marsh was when she died. Not as heartbreakingly young as the children buried here, but certainly not yet old. In the middle, that's what she was. In the middle of raising her family (*Beloved Mother* on her tombstone) and then what? Death, of course, but how? Was it childbirth? He thinks that she was doing something in the service of her family, that she was healthy until the moment she died, and then succumbed to an accident or a sudden insult to the body. He also thinks she had bright red hair that she wore up, and tiny tendrils escaped to frame her face, which pleased both her and her husband. He feels he *knows* this.

It is happening more and more often, this kind of thing. It is happening more and more that when he stands beside a grave, his hat in his hand, part of a person's life story reaches him like the yeasty scent from the bakery he passes every day on his way to the bus stop. He stares at the slightly depressed earth over Adelaide's grave and here comes the pretty white lace dress she loved best, the inequality in the size of her eyes so light brown they were almost yellow. Tea-colored. It comes that her voice was high and clear, that she was shy to sing for her husband, but did so anyway. She did it at night, after they'd gone to bed; the night before she died, she lay in the darkness beside him and sang "Jeannine, I Dream of Lilac Time."

And now this: she had a small diamond ring that was her mother's engagement ring, and Adelaide wore it on a thin gold chain around her neck. It was too small for her finger, and besides, she wanted to keep it close to her heart. Her knuckles were reddened from bleach, her back bothered her from bending over the washtub to scrub her children clean, but she would let no one else do it; she loved the sight of them wet, their curly hair now plastered straight against their skulls, their cheeks pinkened by the warmth of the water; she loved the way she could hold them close for a long time, like babies, when they stepped out of the water and into her arms, into the blue towel she opened to them like a great bird spreading its wings. No. The towel was not blue. What color was it?

What color was it?

Nothing. That's it for today. Arthur puts his hat back on his head, tips it toward Adelaide Marsh's headstone, and moves along. Horace Newton. Estelle McNeil. Irene Sutter. Amos Hammer.

When he reaches Nola's grave, Arthur opens his fold-up chair and gingerly sits down. The legs of the chair sink a little way into the earth, and he steadies himself, making sure the thing won't move any more before he spreads his lunch out onto his lap. An egg salad sandwich he has today, real eggs and real mayonnaise, his doctor be damned. And a liberal sprinkling of salt, as long as he was at it.

Often his doctor can tell when he's been cheating, but not always. Once Arthur ate a whole apple pie covered with vanilla ice cream, and at his appointment the next day, his doctor said, "I'm pleased with your progress, Arthur; whatever you're doing, keep it up. You'll live to be one hundred."

Arthur is eighty-five years old. He guesses he does want to live to be one hundred, even without Nola. It's not the same without her, though. Not one thing is the same. Even something as simple as looking at a daffodil, as he is doing now — someone has planted double-flowered daffodils at the base of a nearby headstone. But seeing that daffodil with Nola gone is not the same, it's like he's seeing only part of it.

The earth has begun softening because of spring. The earth is softening and the buds are all like tiny little pregnant women. Arthur wishes Nola were like spring; he wishes she would come back again and again. They wouldn't even have to be together; he just wants her presence on Earth. She could be a baby reborn into a family far away from here, he wouldn't even have to see her, ever; he would just like to know that she'd been put back where she belongs. Wherever she is now? That's the wrong place for Nola Corrine, the Beauty Queen.

Arthur hears a crow call, and looks around to find the bird. It's sitting on a headstone a few yards away, preening itself.

"*Caw!*" Arthur says back, taking conversation where he finds it, but the crow flies away.

Arthur straightens and regards the cloudless sky, a near-turquoise color today. He puts his hand to the back of his neck and squeezes it, it feels good to do that. He squeezes his neck and looks out over the acres and acres of graves, and nobody here but him. It makes him feel rich.

Arthur takes a bite of his sandwich. Then he gets off his chair and kneels before Nola's headstone, presses his hand against it and closes his eyes. He cries a little, and then he gets back into his chair and finishes his sandwich.

He is folding up his chair, getting ready to go when he sees a young woman sitting on the ground, her back against a tree. Spiky black hair, pale skin, big eyes. Jeans all ripped like the kids do, T-shirt that looks like it's on a hanger, the way it hangs on her. The girl ought to have a coat, or at least a sweater, it's not that warm. She ought to be in school.

He's seen her here before. She sits various places, never near any particular grave site. She never looks at him. She stares out ahead of herself, picking at her nails. That's all she does. Fourteen? Fifteen? He tries waving at her today, but when she sees him she puts her hand to her mouth, as though she's frightened. He thinks she's ready to run, and so he turns away.

Maddy was half asleep when she saw that old man look over at her and wave. When he did, her hand flew up to her mouth and he turned away, then shuffled off with his little fold-up chair. She hadn't meant to do that, make him think she was afraid. Things don't come out right. If she sees him again, she'll ask him who's in the grave. His wife, she imagines, though you can't be sure.

Maddy watches as the old man gets smaller in the distance. She sees him go to the bus stop outside the gate and stand still, staring straight ahead. He doesn't crane his neck, looking to see if the bus is coming. He wouldn't be one of those people who punch an elevator button over and over, Maddy thinks. He'd just wait.

She takes out her phone and snaps a close-up of a tuft of grass, a patch of bark. She loosens her shoelaces, steps out of her shoe, and photographs it lying on its side. She walks to a nearby grave and photographs the center of one of the lilies in the wilting bouquet placed over it, the gently arcing stamens, the upright pistil.

She looks at her watch: 1:40. She'll stay here until school is over, then go home. Tonight, she'll meet Anderson, after he's done working. Anderson is so handsome, he makes you vacant-headed. She met him at the Walmart, where he works in the stockroom. She was leaving the store and he was coming out of the bathroom and he smiled at her and asked if she was Katy Perry. As if. She smiled back. He was on his way to get a hot dog and he asked her to join him. She was scared to, but she did. They didn't talk much, but they agreed to meet later that night. Three months now. She knows some things about him: he was in the Army, he loves dogs, he plays guitar, a little. Once he brought her a gift: a pearl on a gold chain, which she never takes off.

She slides farther down on the tree she's leaning against and makes the space between her knees an aperture. All those graves. Click.

Most people find graveyards sad. She finds them comforting. She wishes her mother had been buried here, and not cremated. Once she heard a guy on the radio say that the cities of the dead are busy places, and it was one of those moments when it felt like a key to a lock. They *are* busy places.

Last time she saw Anderson, she tried to tell him that. They were at a nearly deserted McDonald's, and she spoke quietly. She told him about the old man she saw there all the time, about how he talked to dead people. She told him what the man on the radio had said. She told him she found it peaceful being in a cemetery with the dead. Beautiful, even. What did Anderson think?

"I think you're fucking weird," he said.

It made her go cold in the back. At first she sat motionless in the booth, watching him eat his fries. Then she said, "I know, right?" and barked out a kind of laugh. "Can I have one of your fries?" she asked, and he said, "If you *want* some, *get* some," and shoved a couple of dollars over at her.

But there was the necklace. And one time right after he met her, he sent her a little poem in the mail: *Hope this little note will do / To tell you that I'm missing you.* Another time he kissed her from the top of her head all the way to her toes. All in a long line, kiss, kiss, kiss. She had thought of it the next night at dinner and had had to hide a shiver. "*Eat,*" her father had said. That was one of their chatty dinners, he talked to her. He said a word. Usually, they said nothing. Each had learned the peril of asking questions and getting answers that were essentially rebuffs. "How was work, Dad?" "Work is work." "How was school, Maddy?" "Meh." "Do you like this chicken?" "It's fine." "Want to watch *Game of Thrones* tonight?" "You can."

She checks her watch again, and gets up to find another place to sit.

When Arthur gets home, he pulls the mail from the box, brings it into the kitchen to sort through it, then tosses it all in the trash: junk mail. A waste of the vision he has left, going through it.

He pours himself a cup of cold coffee from the pot on the stove and sits at the kitchen table to drink it, his long legs crossed. He and Nola, they drank coffee all day long. He pauses mid-sip, wondering suddenly if that helped do her in; she had at one time been warned against an excess of caffeine.

He finishes the coffee and rinses out his cup, turns it upside down in the drainer. He uses the same tan-colored cup with the green stripe all the time: for coffee, for water, for his occasional nip of Jack Daniel's, even for his Metamucil. Nola liked variety in all things; he doesn't care, when it comes to dishes. Or clothes. Get the job done, that's all.

Here comes Gordon the cat, walking stiff-legged toward him but looking about for Nola. Still. "She's not here," Arthur tells him, and pats his lap, inviting the cat to jump up. Sometimes Gordon will come, but mostly he wanders off again. Arthur has heard that elephants grieve, seems like cats do, too. Houseplants, too, for that matter. Ironically, he has no luck with them. He looks over at the African violet on the windowsill. Past hope. Tomorrow, he'll throw it away. He says that every day, that he'll do it tomorrow. She had loved the ruffled petals. "Look," she'd told him, when she brought it home, and she'd put a finger under one of the blossoms like it was a chin.

After a dinner of canned stew that looks like dog food, he heads upstairs to the unevenly made bed. She'd be pleased he does that, makes the bed. Here's the big surprise: he's pleased, too. A man doesn't always make room in his life for appreciating certain things that seem to be under women's auspices, but there's a satisfaction in some of them. The toilet seat, though. Up. And there are other grim pleasures in doing things he didn't used to get to do. Cigar right at the kitchen table. Slim Jims for dinner. What he wants on TV, all the time.

He lies down and thinks about that young girl. He feels bad for having scared her. A wave, and she seemed horrified. Seems like he understands more about the dead than the living these days, but he thinks he understands a little about her. If he sees her again, he'll shout over, "Didn't mean to scare you!" Maybe she'll shout back, "I wasn't scared! I wasn't *scared*, get *you*!" The image of her sauntering over to him, her thumbs in her belt loops, looking to pass the time. They could talk. He could introduce her to a few of the folks underground—who *he* thinks they were—if she wouldn't think he was crazy. Maybe she wouldn't think he was crazy; from the looks of it, she has her own strange ways. He might ask her if it didn't hurt, that ring in her nose, hanging out the bottom like a booger.

Arthur sleeps so long the next morning that when he wakes up, it's time for lunch. He sits at the edge of the bed to write the alphabet in the air with his feet, as his doctor has told him to do, to help with the arthritis there. Damned if it doesn't work, too. He heads down to the kitchen. A draft is blowing in from under the door. It's cold and windy then. Odd for May, but who can count on the weather anymore? Never mind. He'll feed Gordon and go. A promise is a promise, even if it's only one you made to yourself.

When he looks in the drawer for the can opener, he doesn't see it. No one to blame it on; he's the only one here. He shifts around the contents of the drawer, then digs deeper, and from way in the back he pulls out Mr. and Mrs. Hamburger. Lord. She kept it. He stares at the molded plastic figurine, all perky beneath the grime: the long-lashed, pink-cheeked Mrs. Hamburger, wearing a red dress with yellow polka dots, Mr. Hamburger in his dark brown suit with a derby hat perched on his bun head. Great big black shoes like Mickey Mouse's for him, chunky red high heels for her. Mrs. Hamburger used to have real hoop earrings; they're gone now. The Hamburgers' skinny white arms— they look like fat pipe cleaners—are linked; they look ready to walk off the stand they're on.

Nineteen fifty-five? Nineteen fifty-six? It was after the Korean war, he knows. He remembers the night they got it, too hot to cook so they went out to the Tick-Tock Diner and he'd bought her that figurine on their way out. It had taken Nola a long time to decide between Mr. and Mrs. Hamburger and Mr. and Mrs. Hot Dog.

They'd had a fight before they left for dinner, he recalls now. They never did fight much, but that one was a doozy. He doesn't remember what it was about, but he sure remembers it. She was just screeching at him, he'd never heard that voice before, and the veins in her neck were standing out. He remembers thinking that he had never seen her look ugly, but he thought she looked ugly then. He doesn't like that he thought that about her, but what can you do? Everybody has thoughts that shame them. You can't control them coming in. But you don't have to let them all out. That's the crux of it. That's what made for civilization, what was left of it, anyway.

He puts the figurine at the center of the kitchen table and stands back to regard it, his hands on his hips. Nola and her figurines. Her little flowered plates and her stationery with birds and apple blossoms. She was a cornball, that one. But who didn't love her?

"Well. Miss *Harris*," Mr. Lyons, Maddy's English teacher, says when she walks into class. That's all he says, but Maddy knows the rest. He knows she skipped school yesterday; he knows she wasn't ill. He leans back in his chair and crosses his arms and watches as she takes her seat.

Mr. Lyons's first name is Royal. Maddy thinks that's hysterical. She wishes she could ask him what's up with that. *Royal.* He's got white hair and he's a little fat. Maddy likes people who are a little fat; it seems to her that they are approachable. He's a little fat and he's got awfully pale skin and the links of his wristwatch are twisted like bad teeth. He doesn't care about such things. He cares about words. He taught her one of her favorite words: *hiraeth,* a Welsh word that means a homesickness for a home you cannot return to, or that maybe never was; it means nostalgia and yearning and grief for lost places. He used the word in a story that he read aloud to the class, and when he looked up, his eyes were full of tears. Nobody made fun of him after class, which was a miracle. Nobody said anything to her, anyway. Not that they would. She's the girl who sits alone in the lunchroom, acting like her sandwich is fascinating. Or did. She skips lunch now.

She doesn't exactly know why kids don't like her. She's good-looking enough. She has a sense of humor. She's not dumb. She guesses it's because they can sense how much she needs them. They are like kids in a circle holding sticks, picking on the weak thing. It is in people, to be entertained by cruelty.

Maddy slides low in her desk so that Mr. Lyons won't call on her today. It's an unspoken agreement they have, another reason she likes him so much. She'd come to school every day if it were just Mr. Lyons. Once she stayed after class to

THE STORY OF ARTHUR TRULUV 15

show him a photo she took lying under a tree and looking up. Mr. Lyons told her the photo was really good in a no-bullshit way. "Do you have a title for it?" he asked. Maddy shrugged and said, "'Framed Sky'?" and Mr. Lyons smiled and said, "Lovely."

Praise is hard for Maddy to hear; it makes her stomach tighten and blood rush to her head, it makes her overly aware of how tall she is. She'd listened to what Mr. Lyons said with no reaction beyond a quick thanks, but later that afternoon, when she was at home and lying on her bed, she looked at the photo again through his eyes. She looked at his comments this way and then that way. What he said could not be seen as anything but good. So . . . so there. She put the photo in the candy box she keeps at the back of her closet. It's a Whitman's Sampler box; her father told her that was her mother's favorite candy, one of the few things he'd shared about her. Maddy never knew her mother; she died in a car crash two weeks after Maddy was born. She'd been on the way to a doctor's appointment. Maddy's father had come home early from work to drive her, but Maddy had a cold and her mother didn't want to take her out. So she told Maddy's father to stay home with Maddy, she'd drive her-self. Someone who ran a red light drove into her.

Maddy has a photo of her mother in the candy box. It's one she found stuck in the crevice of a bookshelf. She asked her father if she could have it and he stared at it for a long time, then gave it to Maddy. In the photo, Maddy's mother is leaning against a fence post somewhere out in the coun-try, her arms crossed, smiling. She has a red scarf tied in her hair, and she's wearing jeans and a man's white shirt with the sleeves rolled up, untucked. "Where was she?" Maddy had asked her father, and her father had said, "With me." "What were you doing?" Maddy had asked, and her father'd said, "Picnic." Then he had walked away. *Enough*, he was saying. Her father will never talk much about her. Too hard.

Maddy looks like her mother: she has her dark hair, her wide blue eyes, her little cleft in the chin. What she wants to know is if she is like her mother.

Maddy writes poems and takes pictures. Lately, she takes pictures of little things and blows them up big so that she can really see them. In poems, she does the opposite: big things get made small so that she can see them. The interest in these things did not come from her father.

Mr. Lyons is talking about *Hamlet*. Maddy lets her mind wander. She already knows about *Hamlet*. They were given a week to read it and Maddy read it that night. To be, or not to be. Right. That *is* the question.

Arthur shuffles over to the stove and turns the heat on high under leftover beans. Then he *walks* back to the table and *walks* back to the stove. No shuffling. *See, Nola?*

He adds catsup to the beans, maple syrup, raw onion, Tabasco, and bacon bits from a jar, though they aren't bacon at all. He cuts a piece of cornbread, butters it, and lays it on the plate, and, when the beans are warm enough, dumps them over the bread. He opens a bottle of beer and sits down to eat.

Gordon jumps up on the table and stares fixedly at him. "Be my guest," Arthur says, moving the plate closer to the cat, so they can share. Gordon sits with his front paws lined up exactly even and eats daintily from one side of the plate. Then he stops abruptly, shakes his head like someone has sprinkled water on him, jumps off the table, and pads away, his tail held high in disdain. "You try cooking then," Arthur says, "you think it's so easy." Funny how an animal can hurt your feelings when you're all alone.

He thinks about maybe watching television later, but he can't much tolerate it anymore. What with the way people behave on there. He'll probably just take a walk around the block after dinner and hope Lucille Howard is not sitting out on her porch. If she's sitting on her porch, he's a dead man. Lucille taught fourth grade for many years, and she seems to think the world is her classroom. She's a bit didactic for Arthur's tastes, a little condescending. Odd, then, that at the thought of seeing her, his weary old heart accelerates. He supposes it could be an erratic beat, he gets them, but he'd prefer to call it something else. So much of everything is what you call it.

He wets his hair at the kitchen sink, then pulls his comb out of his pocket and holds up a pot for a mirror. The bones of his face protrude; he's gotten so skinny he could take a bath in a gun barrel. But good enough. Good enough.

The cat walks behind him as he makes his way to the door. "You coming?" he asks, holding the door open. Gordon is allowed out as long as it's light outside. He's proven his indifference to hunting, an anomaly Arthur appreciates. The cat doesn't move. "Just seeing me out?" Gordon looks up at Arthur, but keeps still. "I'll be back in half an hour," he says. People say cats don't care, but they do.

When Arthur passes Lucille's house, he keeps his gaze focused straight ahead. No point in inviting it. But she's sure enough out there, and he hears her calling him. "Arthur! Want to come and sit a bit?"

He hesitates, then turns and starts up her walk. Gives her a friendly smile, to boot. He wishes she wouldn't wear a wig, or at least not one that sits so crookedly on her head. It's a distraction. Sometimes he has to restrain himself from reaching over and giving it a little tug, then smacking her knee in a friendly way and saying, "There you go!" But why risk humiliating her?

Arthur thinks that, above all, aging means the abandonment of criticism and the taking on of compassionate acceptance. He sees that as a good trade. And anyway, Lucille makes those snickerdoodles, and she always packs some up for him to take home, and he eats them in bed, which is another thing he can do now, oh, sorrowful gifts.

"Sit right there," Lucille says, indicating the wicker chair Arthur always chooses when he visits with her.

He settles down among the floral pillows: one behind him, one on either side of him, one on his lap. It's an undignified and unmanly way to sit, but what can you do? Arthur will never understand what seems to be a woman's need for so many pillows. Nola had it, too. They had to dig their way into bed every night.

"*Now!*" Lucille says. There is an air of satisfaction in her voice that makes him wary.

"Isn't this nice!" she says.

He nods. "Yes. Thank you."

"My grandniece is pregnant, I just found out," Lucille says.

"Oh, is that so?"

"Yes, and do you know, she's forty years old!"

Arthur doesn't know what to say to this. *Congratulations? Uh-oh?*

"These young people, these days," Lucille says. "They just . . . Well, I just don't understand them."

In his lower gut, Arthur feels a rumbling, sudden and acute. He shifts in his chair.

Lucille's eyes dart over and she says, "Oh, I don't mean to complain. No older generation understands the younger generation, isn't that true? But don't let's complain. Let's endeavor to be grateful and pleasant. Unlike them."

And now the pain becomes more acute. What in the hell did he eat?

He rises, warily. "I'm afraid I'm going to have to leave," he says. "Thanks for . . . Thanks for the visit." His voice is pinched with his efforts to keep control.

"But you've only just gotten here!" Lucille says, and—oh, no, look, there are tears trembling in her eyes, magnified by her glasses.

"I forgot about something," Arthur says.

"What?" Lucille demands.

"Oh . . . long story." He really has to get to a bathroom. He moves cautiously toward the steps.

Lucille rises up to walk beside him, her hands kneading each other, and he detects a faint scent of vanilla. "Well, I just hope I didn't offend you. We're neighbors, Arthur, and we're the only old ones left on the block and I just invite you over to pass the time and I made some orange blossom butter cookies for you and—"

"Another time," Arthur says, and hotfoots it over to his house. He reaches the bathroom just in time. He sits on the john and lets go and here comes Gordon to sit on the threshold, his tail wrapped around him. Now there's a friend.

When Arthur's finished, he washes up and then stands there for a minute, doing a kind of internal surveillance, relishing the expansive relief that comes after recovery from illness, however short its duration. He's okay then. So.

He goes into the living room to lift the blinds and looks over at Lucille's porch. Gone in. Well, it would be foolish to go back now. He's sorry for hurting her feelings, but it would be foolish to go back now. The blue of the sky has faded and the thin clouds are ash-colored. The first stars will be out soon. It comes to him that Nola once asked, "What if the souls of the dead become stars that can always watch over everyone?" That was right before she died, and Arthur answered in a way he still regrets. He kissed her hand—so light, by then, a kind of husk of a hand—and said, "We don't know anything." He doesn't know why he said that except that it's basically true. But he wishes he had answered more eloquently. He wishes he'd have said something to make her think that in the great unknown there was one constant: everything would be all right. He thinks that's basically true, too.

He opens the back door and Gordon slips out. "Hey!" Arthur calls. "Get in here!"

The cat's gone. There's a worry. A man Arthur met on his walk the other day said he had seen a coyote walking along the sidewalk, pretty as you please, and Gordon is old now. How old? Arthur slowly calculates. Fifteen! How did that happen? Fifteen!

"Gordon!" he calls. A movement in the bushes and then Gordon darts out and runs to the driveway, where he lies on his back regarding Arthur.

"Come here," Arthur says, patting his leg.

Nothing.

"Come *here!*" Arthur says. And then, rolling his eyes and lowering his voice to a near whisper, "Come, kitty, kitty."

Nothing.

One last thing he can try. He goes into the house and gets Gordon's bag of treats. He carries it outside and shakes it.

Gordon runs away.

Arthur lets the air out of his cheeks. If he ever gets another pet it will be a dog. Nola picked out Gordon at the shelter when the kitten was barely six weeks old. "*Look* at him!" she kept saying, on the ride home. Arthur wasn't sure what he was supposed to look at, but he knew better than to ask. Gordon—unnamed at that point, though Nola had sug-

gested Precious, which of course Arthur had to put the ki-
bosh on—was just a white kitten with a brown tail. But each
time Nola told him to look, he looked over and said, with a
kind of false proprietary pride, "Yup!" You would have
thought they were driving the baby they never could have
home from the hospital.

Arthur goes inside, but leaves the door propped open.
He'll get into his pajamas and brush his teeth and wash his
face and his glasses, then check again. If the cat doesn't
come back then, well, he's on his own. Bon appétit, coyote.

Arthur finishes his preparations, then comes back downstairs. No sign of Gordon. He calls him once more, then
closes and locks the door and heads upstairs. He opens the
book he's reading, but he can't concentrate. He snaps out
the light, lies down, and stares out into the blackness. When
he feels a thud on the bed, he jumps and cries out, much to
his shame. You'd think a bat had dropped from the ceiling.
But it's only Gordon, the devil.

"Where were you?" Arthur asks. Gordon comes closer,
curls up next to him, and starts purring.

"You think I'm going to pet you now?" Arthur asks. "After
what you put me through?"

But he does pet him. And then he sits up and snaps the
light back on and reads a few pages from his Western before
he goes to sleep, a feeling like an inflated balloon in his
chest, the cat curled in his lap. Little mercies.

———

At midnight, Maddy calls Anderson. She keeps her voice low, so her father won't hear. Anderson answers sleepily, and Maddy instantly regrets herself. But what can she do now except plunge in?

"Hey," she says, but her voice is too girly, so she lowers it to say, "What are you doing?"

"I'm fucking sleeping," Anderson says. "Duh."

"Well, I'm sorry to wake you but you said you were going to call tonight, so . . ."

"Did I? Sorry. But I just saw you, right? And I . . . got busy."

Doing what? she wants to ask, but best not to push. He did apologize.

She starts to ask him about his day but things have gotten to such a bad place. So she asks in what she hopes is a jaunty, playful way, "Want me to sneak out and meet you?"

"I don't know, Maddy," he says, and the distance in his voice terrifies her.

"I learned a new trick," she says, and he laughs and says, "Oh yeah? What trick is that?"

"It's a surprise."

He's quiet, and she says, "Meet me at the corner. We'll go somewhere. I'll do it to you in the car."

He sighs. "I gotta work in the morning. We need to make it fast, okay? Nothing after."

"Okay," she says. "I'll be out there in fifteen minutes. Come and get me."

She hangs up and contemplates what to wear. Something easy to slip off. This is exciting. It is, isn't it? She feels like she's in a television show. But now she needs to think of a trick.

She takes off her pajamas and pulls on a T-shirt. No bra. Jeans, no underpants. Then she uses her phone to google *Variations on oral sex, female to male.*

When it's time, she raises her bedroom window, climbs out into the foundation shrubbery, and crouches down, listening, making sure she has not awakened her father. No; she hears nothing. She walks to the corner to wait. She stands there seven minutes, she counts every second with a despairing kind of dread, but then here come his headlights and the car pulls up next to her. His arm is hanging out through the open window and the smoke from his cigarette is rising up and it's so sexy, it's so right, he's so manly, nothing like the dumb boys in her school, whose idea of a good time is trying to slam locker doors on each other's hands.

She wets her lips, runs to the passenger side, and leaps in. He nods but says nothing, just drives off to a forest preserve a couple of miles away. He pulls into one of the parking spaces, cuts the engine, and turns to face her.

"Hey," he says, and he rubs at the corner of one eye. The gesture is endearing to her, somehow, and she leans over to kiss him. But he pulls away, saying, "I gotta get back soon, I gotta get up early. So, you know. What's up?"

"What's *up?*" she says.

"Yeah, what's the trick?"

"Oh," she says. "Well, so . . . Want me to show you?"

"*Yeah.*"

No need for her to get undressed after all. No time.

She puts her hand to his crotch, unbuttons his jeans, and carefully pulls the zipper down. Apparently there's this little place back there where you can rub when you do it. Apparently they love that. Awkwardly, she gets on her knees on the floor in front of him.

He leans his head back, closes his eyes. Tosses his cigarette out the window. She looks at his handsome face, then begins.

Afterward, she says, "So . . . ?"

"Yeah, it was great. Thanks."

Thanks? "You're welcome," she says. She moves back to her side of the seat.

"Listen, Maddy," he says, looking down, and her insides jump at the sight of his long lashes, the planes of his cheekbones, the way his hair falls into his face.

He looks at her to say, "I gotta tell you. I think we need to cut back on seeing each other."

She freezes. Cannot speak. Does not breathe.

"Okay? I mean, I'm busy at work, and I'm trying . . . you know, I'm trying to do some other stuff."

"What stuff? Something I can help with? I could help you."

"No, it's nothing. . . ." He looks out the side window, then back at her. "Aw, Maddy, I can't lie to you. You're a good kid. You're a pretty girl, we had some good times, right? But you . . . Okay, I'm just going to say it right out because I respect you, okay? Like, I'm not going to lie to you. I found someone. . . . She's more my age, okay?"

"Who is it?" Maddy has no idea why she has asked this

question. Or how. She doesn't want to hear a single word about whoever this person might be.

"She works at the store, we run into each other a lot."

We. It burns. Maddy presses her lips together tightly. *Must not cry. Really must not cry.*

He laughs. "At first we hated each other. It's really funny, it's like a sitcom, right? We like really *hated* each other. This one time she came into—"

"It's okay," Maddy says. "I don't want to hear any more."

"Aw, come here," he says softly, and some force moves her closer to him. Where else can she go?

"Hey. I got something for you." He reaches into his pocket and pulls out a small jewelry box.

Oh, my god. This was a joke! The other girl, that was a joke! Because look, he's going to propose! And she will say yes, she will say, *Just take me to your apartment and we'll start living together right now.* She stares at the box, her heart galloping in her chest. To be out of her house, away from her father, who is like constant bad weather. To wake up excited for the day ahead! To feel seen and appreciated! Maddy feels she wears a mask behind which is a wondrous kaleidoscope. Look through here: she knows things; turn the wheel: she can do things. She can sing, she's a good dancer, she can curl her tongue on demand, every dog and cat on the street comes up to her, she's an amazingly fast reader. Now she can show someone everything: her heart, her humor, her loyalty!

"Take it," Anderson says, pushing the box toward her.

She takes it, her hand shaking, and opens it to find a

pearl solitaire necklace, identical to the one he gave her before.

"A token of my appreciation," he says, as though he were dressed in a tux and bowing before her. "Do you like it?"

She reaches beneath the neckline of her T-shirt to pull out her necklace and shows it to him.

"Oh," he says. "Shit."

She starts to get out of the car and he grabs her arm. "What are you doing?"

She says nothing, tries to wrestle her arm free, and he holds on tighter. It hurts. She turns toward him and slaps his face. It startles both of them, he lets go, and she gets out of the car, leaving the door open. Let him shut it. She starts running away.

"Maddy!" he says. "What in the hell are you doing? Get in the car, I'll give you a ride home. For Christ's sake, get in the *car!*"

She keeps running, faster.

"Maddy! It's not safe!"

She hears him slam the passenger door and the car starts coming toward her. She runs into the woods.

"Maddy!" she hears. And then she hears the car driving off.

She comes out of the woods and there is no sign of him. She waits for a minute to see if he will come back, but he doesn't.

Maybe fifty feet away, just at the periphery of the woods, she notices a doe watching her, and she becomes flooded with an elemental sense of shame. She stares back at the animal, its wide and patient eyes, its stillness. For a long time, neither moves. Then, "Mom?" Maddy whispers.

When she was little, Maddy used to watch Mister Rogers on TV. Her father would set her up on the sofa with animal crackers and juice and disappear into the bedroom or the basement, where he could be alone. Maddy would watch the little train and the puppets and the regular visitors to Mister Rogers' Neighborhood. She would listen to the soothing voice of a man she wished her father were like. One day Mister Rogers stared out from the screen as though he were talking right to her. "Look for the helpers," he advised. "If you look for the helpers, you'll know that there's hope." She'd started when she heard that, then held perfectly still. She wouldn't have been surprised if Mister Rogers had reached out his hand through the screen. She has never forgotten that day, that feeling of being offered some sort of lifeline.

Maddy feels her mother sometimes as a glow in her brain, as a knock at her heart, as a whisper she can't quite hear. And then there are times when she thinks her mother takes on the form of something else, like this doe, appearing from out of the woods to stand by her, if only from a distance. Maddy sees this as wordless reassurance, as fulfillment of the promise that Mister Rogers made, and it does offer her hope, though that hope is not nearly as bright as it used to be. That hope has gotten tired.

Maddy swallows, holds up a hand. "Bye," she says, and starts walking.

When she gets home, she climbs noiselessly through the window and, once inside, turns on her desk lamp. Her father is sitting on the edge of her bed. "Where have you been?" he asks.

There is nothing left in her. She is not afraid.

"I snuck out to meet a boy."

Her father nods. He stares at her standing there, her arms crossed, her heart shattered.

Then, "Come here," he says, and pats the bed beside him. Maddy moves to the place he's indicated and sits staring straight ahead.

Her father clears his throat. He puts his hand over Maddy's, and Maddy's stomach clenches. Her natural response to his rare attempts at affection is to stiffen or move away from him. Because these attempts are not felt as warm. Rather they are felt as foreign and intrusive, and as reminders of what was almost always missing and, at least at first, acutely longed for. Over the years, she has built a little fort against wanting any of that from him anymore. It is too late now. The fort is impenetrable. She is safe inside it.

"Look," her father says. "I know I'm not . . . I know it might not seem so, but I love you. Please don't ever do that again. I was scared, you scared me. Will you promise me never to do that again? That's not the way. Boys don't respect girls who do that. Okay?"

No shit. "Okay," she says, and takes her hand away.

"Don't do it ever again." He looks over at her, starts to speak again, then doesn't. "Good night." He rises, tiredly, it seems to her, tired beyond the lateness of the hour, and, at the threshold, turns around to face her. "Do you want to talk about anything?"

She shakes her head no.

"I'm going grocery shopping tomorrow. Do you need anything?"

"No."

"Are you sure?"

"I said no!"

He hesitates, then again says, "Good night."

"Good night." They are beautiful words, she thinks. Good. Night.

She gets under her covers without undressing. She will not think of him. What did she expect? She will not think of him. She will think of good. And night.

In the morning, she will take the bus to school and then she will not go to school but instead will walk over to the cemetery. To be with her people.

Before he heads to the bus stop, Arthur decides to stop over at Lucille's. He will apologize. He will say that he had been indisposed, and had been embarrassed to say so. But he's okay now, and maybe they can chat that evening. He hopes Lucille will agree, and maybe even say, "Wait just a minute, I'll give you something for your lunch." And then she might come out with a baggie of cookies for him. Orange blossom, he thinks she said last night. Butter orange blossom. They'll be good, he bets. His mouth waters, just thinking of them. Lucille can bake! As she will tell you, but let the woman take credit where credit is due. Sometimes when she bakes her caramel cake he can smell it from his living room.

He crosses over his yard and goes up the steps to her front door. Knocks the shave-and-a-haircut way. He hears her moving around inside and reaches toward the back of his head to smooth his hair down. Puts his hands behind his back, then in front of him. Rocks back on his heels, then forward. Knocks again. Silence this time. He rings the doorbell, but she doesn't come. Is she all right? It's a question that does occur at this age. He rings again, then cracks open the door to say, "Lucille?" and here she comes, rushing up quickly to meet him. Look at the pink in her face. Good.

Only not, because what she says is "What are you doing, opening my door like that? What are you doing?"

"I . . . Well, you didn't answer, and I was afraid you had fallen or something and I—"

"Fallen!"

"Well, yes, Lucille, I was worried you might have fallen."

"I have never fallen in my life since I was a little girl."

"I'm glad to hear that."

They stand there, and then she says, "I have to go."

"Okay. I guess I'll see you, then."

She shuts the door.

So. She's angry. He could knock again and apologize, ask if she'd like to talk. But you know what? He doesn't want to.

He does not want to. What he wants to do is go and have lunch with Nola. It is his greatest pleasure and he doesn't care who knows it.

Still, exiting the porch, he turns around one last time. Maybe he sees the curtain flutter, maybe he doesn't.

He rides the bus a bit subdued, but his heart lifts once he walks through the cemetery gates. It's a beautiful day, puffy white clouds seeming to ride the blue sky. Blue is the right color for a sky, and white is the right color for clouds. His pace picks up. He's brought peanut butter and grape jelly for lunch today, and one of those little fruit cups, and a thermos of milk on account of the peanut butter and jelly. When the day comes when he can no longer enjoy peanut butter and jelly, well, he will be ready to reside in heaven with Nola. He hopes there really is a heaven. He hopes there's a way he can see her again. How he would love to see her again right now! If only he could, he wouldn't tell anyone, it would be his and God's little secret, but, oh, what he wouldn't give to see that face alive again just for an instant, those eyes looking right into his. It would sustain him for the rest of his days.

Ah well.

He starts walking down a row.

Annette McAllister. Dead at eighty. A long life, one might say, though if you asked Annette, she might disagree. Arthur bends slightly over her grave. *Forget-me-nots*, he gets. Must have been her favorite flower. *A bad case of arthritis, knuckles all knobby. A knitter, nonetheless. Peanut brittle in a yellow bowl by her recliner. Irritated by small children.*

Arthur straightens. Irritated! Well, you always want to give the benefit of the doubt to those buried and gone, but Arthur cannot abide those who don't like small children. Oh, maybe little kids are trouble, sometimes, but only for a good reason: They are tired. They are hungry. They are afraid. He supposes a great many ills of adults might be cured by a nap or a good meal or a bit of timely reassurance. But adults complicate everything. They are by nature complicators. They learned to make things harder than they need to be and they learned to talk way too much. Not that he isn't guilty of his own sins, as an adult. His loss of enthusiasm for spontaneity, for one. Nola used to complain about that. "Let's go for a drive!" she'd say, and he'd say, "When?" and she'd say, "*Now!*" "Where?" he'd ask, and she'd say, "Anywhere!" And he'd say, oh, he couldn't right then. Finally, she stopped asking, because he always said he couldn't do it right then. But he could have! He could have and should have. You ask kids if they want to go for a drive, what do they say? Yes! Want to catch minnows? Yes! Want to bury treasure? Yes! Want to spin around and get dizzy? Yes! The truth is that, apart from Nola, Arthur always has favored being with kids over adults.

Arthur moves on toward Nola's row. Passes Harold Lawton. Passes Henry Olson. Passes Heidi Mueller and pauses. *Born March 14, 1922. Died December 25, 2011.* Christmas Day. That must have been a hard one. He stands still, his fists clenched. *War bride,* he thinks. *Came here with her soldier husband. War bride with blond curly hair and the bluest eyes. She stood and watched, from behind lace curtains, as an*

Army convoy rolled into her town at the end of World War II. The Nazis had told the women not to talk to the Americans, who would try to rape them, who would give them chocolate laced with poison. She talked to a soldier anyway. He had three new toothbrushes in his front pocket. She saw them and she wanted one, because luxury had come to this: a new tooth-brush. He'd begged a kiss in exchange; she refused; he was smitten. He was from New York City, nearly undone by all he had witnessed in the war, and the sight of this woman was a rose in snow. He was fined for breaking the fraternization ban and talking to her. Never mind. Just one look, that's all it took.

Just one look, it happens more often than people think. Happened with him and Nola. He looked at her standing at the candy counter at the dime store and everything inside him took the express elevator down, then up, zip-a-dee-doo-dah. "Miss?" he'd said, around the lump in his throat. She'd turned toward him and smiled, and he'd said, "I'm going to marry you." And she hadn't run away. She'd said, "When?"

Arthur looks up at the sky, which has suddenly darkened. Rain wasn't forecast, but apparently the rain didn't check the forecast. He'll eat quickly, bless the resting spot of his wife, whose spirit glows in him and around him still and forever, and then he'll head home. He'll plant the tomato seeds he bought to start in little Dixie cups. It makes him feel like the Lord above when those things sprout. A man may not have a whole vegetable garden, but a man needs his fresh tomatoes in the summer.

He sits down on his fold-up chair and is just about to start in on his lunch when he sees that girl again. She's watching him, her back against a tree, her arms crossed. Her backpack is beside her. It's one o'clock. Why isn't she in school?

Tentatively, he raises his hand and waves. She waves back, then stands and starts over toward him. Her gait is slow but purposeful, her expression unreadable.

When she reaches him, he stands and says, "Well, hello there."

"You come here all the time," she says.

"And you almost as often."

She shrugs. Then, gesturing with her chin to Nola's grave. "That your wife?"

Arthur nods. "That's Nola. She died six months ago. Nola Corrine, the Beauty Queen."

Silence, as they both regard the headstone, and then Arthur says, "I miss her an awful lot, and so I come out here to have lunch with her every day. Feels like I'm having lunch with her."

"Was she a beauty queen?"

"To me, she was."

"You talk to her, right?" Maddy says. It is a child's question, innocent and absent of judgment.

"Yes, I do."

"What do you talk to her about?"

He straightens, offers a smile.

"It's private; okay, I get it," Maddy says, and Arthur sees that she's embarrassed, a little folded in on herself. She's a fragile one, this one.

"It's not so private," he says. "I talk out loud. Anyone

nearby could hear me, if they wanted to. In fact, I guess you might have heard me at one time or another."

She shakes her head. "I never heard you. I saw your mouth moving, but I never heard you."

"Well, it's nothing very much," Arthur says. "I tell her what I've been up to. I tell her anything that comes into my head, really. The weather. Sometimes a story I read in the paper, something funny; she used to like the funny things or the human interest stories, she didn't care for politics." He looks into the girl's face, sees the dark rings under her eyes. "Sometimes I tell her how much I miss her. Though that's . . . Well, that's like trying to put an elephant through the eye of a needle. If you know what I mean."

Maddy nods.

"I'm Arthur Moses," he says, and offers his hand. She looks at it, then shakes it, and Arthur isn't sure that she's ever shaken a hand before. He supposes it's possible. It's not something you see young people doing a lot. Seems like they mostly keep their hands in their pockets, something that used to be considered rude. That or they're type-type-typing on their phones.

"Maddy Harris," the girl says.

A crack of thunder, and then the rain starts suddenly. Fat drops land on Arthur's neck, run down the back of his shirt. He hunches his shoulders, speaks loudly over the noise of the storm. "Looks like we got a monsoon here! Guess I'd better go!"

"Yeah," she says.

He starts to walk away, and the rain intensifies; it's the kind of rain that hits the headstones so hard it bounces up.

"Hey!" he says, turning back to where the girl is standing. "There's a bus coming in just a few minutes. Would you like to come over to my house and get out of the rain?"

"Arthur!" Nola used to say, about such sudden impulses. Once they had just bought a loaf of cinnamon indulgence bread and he gave half of it away to a passerby who said it smelled good. And when Nola widened her eyes at him as he walked away with her, he said, "What. Last time we gave half the loaf to the birds."

"Yes, and the birds like it!" Nola said. "And I like to give it to them!"

Arthur licked a little cinnamon sugar off his pointer finger. Then he offered it to Nola. She frowned ferociously but then laughed and had a lick herself. That was Nola for you, couldn't hold a grudge if you paid her.

Arthur tells Maddy, "We have to hurry if you want to come."

She doesn't move. She stands looking at him and he sees in her eyes when she makes her decision. She hikes her backpack up onto her shoulder and says something he can't hear.

"Pardon?"

"I said, 'Fine, I like riding the bus.'"

They walk quickly through sudden mud toward the stop. Arthur hopes Lucille won't see him bringing this girl into the house. Then he hopes she does see them. Maybe she'll come over with cookies. Though Lucille very rarely comes over. Almost always, he goes to her house, and usually just as far as the porch, though he does help her put her star on top of her Christmas tree. Isn't it funny. All the years they've lived next to each other and so rarely do they cross each other's thresholds. He liked it better when he was a kid and he and his friends ran into and out of each other's houses as though they lived in all of them.

He and the girl reach the bus stop and Arthur is relieved; his heart feels odd, like it's shimmying. He's out of breath. He would like to sit down on his chair, but some old relic of masculinity makes him refuse. But then the girl takes the chair from him, opens it, and gestures for him to sit there. And he does. And then they wait in silence in the pouring rain for the bus.

Arthur realizes that if he were alone, it would be a grim wait. With the girl, it is an adventure. That's what being with another does. He remembers now with something like a full-body flush, he remembers what it means to share something with someone, the particular alchemy that can light things up.

If Lucille doesn't see them go into his house, he'll go and get her. As long as he's collecting women.

"Here it comes," Maddy says, and Arthur sees the bus approaching, headlights on, windshield wipers slapping at high speed. So much water has collected already in the gutters that the bus looks part boat.

"Oh, wait, I don't have any *money*," Maddy says. "Will you lend me some?"

"I'll pay," he says. "I've got a monthly pass."

When they board the bus, the driver won't let Maddy ride on Arthur's card. "Are you kidding?" Arthur says.

"She doesn't qualify," the driver says. He's a mean old bird, squinty eyes, no sense of humor or compassion.

"I'll pay, then," Arthur says, and digs in his pocket for the fare. Luckily, he's a man who believes in carrying change around.

"Thank you," Maddy says, her head bowed.

They sit in the handicap seat, just behind the driver, since he's not going to wait for them to find any other seat.

"How far are we going?" Maddy asks.

"Seventeen blocks," Arthur says. "We'll be at my house in ten minutes. Do you like soup?"

"What kind?"

"Bean and bacon?"

She wrinkles her nose.

"Tomato?"

"Yes. Thank you." She turns to stare out the window, and Arthur sneaks a look at her reflection. Such a sad face.

When they arrive at Arthur's stop, the rain has let up. They make the short walk to his house, and it is only as they are heading up the steps to go in that the girl hesitates.

It occurs to Arthur to ask if she would like to just sit on the porch, but here comes the sound of Gordon meowing on the other side of the door.

"Do you have a cat?" Maddy asks.

Arthur nods. "Gordon. He gets mad if I leave him. Though of course he'll walk away when I come in."

He puts the key to the lock and opens the door. Gordon looks up at him, sees the girl, and freezes.

"This is Maddy," Arthur says, and, to her, "Come on in."

She steps through the door and Arthur closes it behind her. She takes off her muddy boots, reminding Arthur to take off his shoes as well. Maddy's socks have skulls on them; Arthur's have holes in both toes. He wasn't expecting company.

The girl starts to shrug out of her jacket and Arthur goes behind her to help her.

"What are you *doing?*" Maddy says, spinning around.

"I was going to help you with your jacket."

"I can get my own jacket off."

"Sorry. I'm just used to doing that. Gentlemen used to do that, help a lady with her coat. Open doors for them. You know. You've seen it in *movies,* haven't you?"

"It smells like onions in here," Maddy says.

"Well," Arthur says.

"I like onions." She stoops down and Gordon walks right up to her. He sticks his big head under her hand and closes his eyes when she scratches him.

"I guess *you've* got a friend," Arthur says.

"Well, that makes one."

"Two," Arthur says.

She looks up at him quickly. And then she collapses onto the floor and puts her hands over her face.

"Uh-oh," Arthur says. "Maddy? Are you . . . ?"

Well, he can't get down there with her, he'll never get up again.

"Maddy?"

She pulls her hands down and looks at him. "I got dumped last night."

Arthur nods. Then, "Huh," he says. "Me, too."

She frowns. "Really?"

"I think so. Let's have lunch, and you tell me what you think. And then I'll tell you what I think. About your story. About what happened to you. If you'll tell me."

Maddy pushes herself up off the floor, wiping at her nose. Arthur winces, imagining how it must tug at the ring. "I'll tell you *some*," she says.

"Good enough." Arthur goes into the kitchen and sneaks a glance over into Lucille's house. Nothing. Dark. She must be out. He hopes she brought an umbrella.

Arthur pulls out a chair for Maddy at the table. "I'll just get this ready," he says. He hopes he has enough milk for the soup. He hopes he has two matching bowls. He hopes they're clean. When you live alone, you become a lot more tolerant of certain things.

"Is there a *drawer* in this table?" Maddy asks.

"Yup. That's the way they used to do it. And they would keep silverware in there. Convenient! Nola and I used to keep our Green Stamps in it. 'Course they don't have them anymore."

"What are green stamps?"

"Oh, you'd collect them at the grocery store or gas stations and then you could trade them in for things. Dishes. Toys. Save enough and you could even get some real nice furniture. Little kids used to love pasting the stamps into the books."

"Did your kids?"

"I don't . . . We couldn't have any kids, Nola and I."

"You're better off," Maddy says, low.

"What's that?"

"I said, 'You're better off'!"

Arthur pulls his head out of the refrigerator to stare at her. "Now why in the world would you say that?"

She shrugs.

"Don't you like kids?"

"*I* do. But a lot of other people don't. A lot of people have no idea what to do with kids. Seems like they think they're just in the way."

Arthur finds the milk and shakes the carton. There's enough for the soup. He opens the can and dumps the contents into the pan. Then he adds the milk, his hand shaking a little bit. "I wish I'd had kids for lots of reasons, but especially now I wish I had them."

Silence, and then, "How old are you?" Maddy asks, and Arthur tells her eighty-five. Then he asks her how old she is.

"Eighteen," she says. "Almost."

Eighteen. The word is a poem. "You don't look eighteen," he tells her.

"I know. When I was *born*, I looked young for my age."

He hesitates, then laughs. And she smiles. Good Lord, he's never seen such a smile. It's like the sun came out in her face. Such a pretty girl, if she'd just take that thing out of her nose.

"Do you have any bread?" Maddy asks.

"Sure. Half a loaf."

"Do you have any cheese?"

"I got some American slices."

"Want me to make us some toasted cheese croutons for the soup?"

He frowns. "How do you make those?"

"I never made them, but I saw in a restaurant they had tomato soup with toasted cheese croutons. I guess you just make a toasted cheese sandwich and cut it up."

"Okay with me," Arthur says. "Get yourself a frying pan." He gestures with his foot toward the bottom cupboard.

She gets out a little cast-iron pan. "Do you have any butter?"

"If you won't tell my doctor, I do."

It's eleven-thirty by the time Lucille lets herself into her house. Eleven-thirty! Practically midnight! She hasn't been up this late in years!

But oh.

She prepares for bed as two people. Here is the Lucille that she is now, creaming off her face, but also here is the Lucille she was then, her cheeks full and pink, her skin dewy, her shoulder-length hair chestnut-colored and so thick she could barely get a brush through it. Not only does she see her face—*oh! she was pretty!*—but she feels her young body as well. It's true, she can feel herself as she was then! Her chin lifts, her legs straighten, and she feels a rush of vitality running from the top of her head to the bottom of her feet as startling as if someone had dumped a bucket of water on her. Or like that time she stuck a fork in the toaster before it popped up.

She presses her lips together, puts her fingers to her mouth, and squeezes her eyes shut. Feels something between a laugh and a cry come out of her. She shuts off the bathroom light and makes her way to her bed. *Walking on clouds*, she really understands what that means now.

She lies down, turns out the bedside lamp, and sees his face in the darkness. His two faces, his young one, from when she was with him, and his old face, the man he has become. Guess which face is bigger. Guess which face hangs in the air before her like a big fat moon.

Frank Pearson.

Frank Pearson!

"I thought you were dead," she told him. And he said, "I thought you were, too," and his eyes were full of wonder. You can say all you want about chocolate and flowers. Never mind all that. To be alive when you were thought gone! To be alive and well! Well enough, anyway.

Lucille sighs. She's exhausted, but she's not sure she'll be able to sleep. She clasps her hands over her abdomen, tries to slow her breathing. Then her eyes pop open.

She's going on a diet. She's contemplated doing it before, for health reasons, because every time she visits the doctor, he looks at her weight on the chart and then up at her and Lucille says, "I know very well what you're going to say. I will lose the weight." That's what she says every time she sees Dr. Fink. Every time. But losing weight for health reasons is a very dull prospect, doomed at the outset. Losing weight for romance, that's altogether different.

Tomorrow she was going to stuff pieces of Kraft caramels into chocolate chip cookie bars. She guesses she won't do that now, although she was very curious about how that would taste. Maybe she'll make them anyway and give them all to Arthur. That man is so skinny he disappears if you look at him sideways. Yes, she'll give everything she bakes to him, he'll be thrilled. She's not mad at Arthur anymore, because of Frank. Smile, and the world smiles with you. All the world loves a lover.

She lies there and tries to shut off her mind, but it's no use; she can't sleep. She turns the light back on, slides into her slippers, and goes downstairs to get the letter she received just the other day. And they say nobody gets letters anymore. Well, she got a letter and it was something else. What if it had gotten lost? What if it had blown out of her hand? What if despite the handwritten address she had thought it was junk mail, as most of her mail is, and had thrown it out? What if she'd looked at the return address and said, *Oh no you don't, it's way too late for you and me!* Which it is. But it's not.

She brings the envelope back to bed with her and unfolds the single page. She'd had a hard time reading his penmanship at first, but she can read it now lickety-split. The truth is, she has memorized the letter, but it's better to read it, to examine again the way the *g*'s hang open, the way the *t*'s are crossed with emphatic slanted lines. The way he underlined *hope*, that's her favorite.

She reads the letter again and then tucks it under her pillow. She doesn't think he's happy he dumped her all those many years ago for Sue Benson. Who *died* a year ago. Died! From leukemia! In just three months! But anyway, she doesn't think he was ever happy he married her. He'd had to, that's all. He'd had a fling with Sue after he went to a party without Lucille. Sue was all over him, he gave in to her, and presto, a bun in the oven. And then so many years later, here he comes a-calling.

Oh, she remembers something now. He used to do this thing where he turned her hand over and very, very gently kissed her palm, then her wrist, then her lips.

They make a lip plumper that you can get right at the drugstore, anyone can buy it, she saw it the other day when she was getting her prescriptions filled. And she'd thought, *What foolishness*, and she'd loosened her dress from where it had gotten stuck to her thighs a little, which happens all the time; she has to be mindful.

She needs to find her half-slips, which she never threw away as far as she can recall; they must be around here somewhere. She once had a full slip that was a mint green, and it had tea-colored lace in abundance at the bodice and all along the bottom, beautiful lace, it practically made your mouth water, and she had bought it for her hope chest and then never used it, of course, but she bets that slip is around here, too.

Naturally it won't fit now, but she *is* going on a diet. Not that Frank said anything about her being so much heavier than when he knew her. He wasn't exactly a GQ model himself. But now it's not just vanity; now she really does want to live longer, because she has been reminded that you never know. You just never know.

It seems to be in vogue for gerontologists to ask their patients if they want to live to be a hundred. She's been asked that a few times. Always, she says, "Well, of course!" because she thinks that's the right answer. You can't tell these people the truth. When her ninety-year-old friend Franny Miller told her doctor, "No, I certainly do *not* want to live to be a hundred; I don't even want to live to be ninety-one!" she got a mental health referral. *For heaven's sake,* Lucille used to think, whenever she was asked that question, *why in the world would I want to live to a hundred?* Now, because of this one thing that has happened, which is kind of a miracle, it really is, she does want to live that long! People are living much longer in relatively good health. She saw a man in Denny's the other day who might have been *more* than a hundred, and he was putting down pancakes like it was a competition sport. And he walked out with nary so much as a cane. Bent over, okay, moving slowly, okay, but walking completely independently. She herself is only eighty-three, only four years out of her seventies; think of all she can do!

She gets out of bed and goes downstairs to pack up all the orange blossom cookies for Arthur. She has those cute Chinese take-out containers, only they're for cookies. Her grandniece sent them to her, probably hoping Lucille would use them to send baked goods to her. But Lucille fits all the cookies into three boxes for Arthur. All except for two of them, which she pops into her mouth, both at once, get it over with. *They* won't hurt. Just two. My goodness, they are good. My *goodness!* She slips her hand under the flap of one of the boxes to get one more. If she doesn't open the box all the way, it doesn't count.

Across the way, she sees the light on in Arthur's kitchen. He's probably eating packaged cookies. She sneaks closer to the window and peers over. Yup. She doesn't think his wife ever baked cookies, that Nola. She was a nice enough woman, but she seemed to find all she needed in her husband. But now he's adrift, isn't he, just sitting over there eating Double Stuf Oreos that they never should have double-stuffed, what were they thinking? She bets Arthur misses her cookies like crazy. Just like a man, doesn't know how much he needs you until he sees how much he needs you.

Cherise Baumgartner. Born March 19, 1943. Died August 9, 2016. Oh, this one. This one was a librarian, the prettiest thing you ever saw in spectacles. A mole perched at the angle of her jaw. Flame red hair and sea green eyes. Favored the color pink. Wore her hair up in a bun that always immediately started falling down in a most attractive way. Had no time for the fact that she was so pretty, didn't like that she was so pretty, told her mother at ten years old that she wished people would stop saying she was so pretty. When she read, she liked to be barefoot and she liked to lace her fingers through her toes. Never married. Too busy reading, she used to tell people who harped on that.

Opal Erickson, beloved daughter, sister, aunt. And then—oddly, Arthur thinks, for these words are etched toward the bottom of the stone in a different font—there is this: *Friend / Cherished in life / Loved beyond death.*

He stands with his sack lunch in one hand, his fold-up chair in the other, thinking. What could it mean? *Friend,* he doesn't think he's ever seen that before. Was she gay? He checks the dates on the headstone. Born 1905, died 1980. He supposes she could have been. He closes his eyes, and inclines his head closer to the grave. Nothing. Opal's not talking, at least not to him.

He walks on, and a few graves down he feels what is almost a tug at his sleeve:

Cal Bierman. Born June 1, 1900. Died July 4, 1990. A trout fisherman, a man made philosopher by the sound of rushing water. Parted his hair right smack down the middle, fashionable or not. A reddened, bulbous nose but a temperate drinker. Never liked to talk about it, but he fainted on his wedding day right at the altar in front of everyone. Favored basset hounds. His favorite holiday was the Fourth of July and he and his immediate and then extended family had a big picnic every year in honor of it. Even in old age, he and his wife would load up the car with blankets and lawn chairs and go out to reserve a place in the park while the sky was still a smoky red and the birds had not yet begun to sing. How fitting then, the day that he died.

Well. Time's a-wasting. He brought tuna fish today, and it's warm out. Better eat it. Tuna fish and a couple of tangerines and orange blossom cookies, and he might just eat them first. He meant to bring four cookies, but another one slid in. Lucille outdid herself with these. He's glad she's not mad at him anymore. She's not as friendly as she was, but she's not mad.

A few days ago, he was pruning the Juneberry tree in the side yard when he saw her on her porch getting her mail. "Hello!" he called out.

She held her hand up in a kind of lackluster way, the equivalent of saying, *Yeah, so?*

"Are you free for dinner tonight?" he asked, and was aware of a peculiar nervousness. It had been a long time since he'd asked a woman on a date.

"What did you say?" she asked, kind of irritably, he thought, and he repeated the question.

"Why are you asking?" she said.

He put his hand on his hip, cocked his head. "Why am I asking?"

"Yes, why are you asking me? Since I'm such a bore to you."

"Lucille, I apologize about that, about the other night."

"What?"

He sighed, walked over to stand beneath her porch railing. "I said I apologize about the other night. I was . . . feeling indisposed."

"Then why did you come over in the first place?"

He looked away, then back. "It came on suddenly, Lucille. Okay? Came on real suddenly and I had to get home fast."

The light dawned in her face. "Oh. Well, you should have said so."

"I'm saying so now and I'm also asking you to go out with me tonight and have dinner."

"Where?"

"I thought maybe the Olive Garden? The bus stops right in front."

"I have a car, Arthur."

"I thought you don't like to drive at night."

She hesitated, tapping the mail absentmindedly against her thigh.

"All right. But I'm paying for my*self*!"

"Well!" Arthur said. "*That*'ll teach me."

But in the end, he paid for everything, the bus, the meal, everything. They made up, and he was surprised at the relief he felt.

Lucille's been gone a lot in the evenings, he never much sees her on the porch anymore when he takes his walks. She didn't say anything about it at their dinner, and he didn't want to bring it up, lest she tell him it was none of his business. But last night he saw her get into a car, a big red Cadillac, no less! He couldn't make out the driver, and then figured it could very well be that she had family in town. That happened now and then, she'd be off every night and then, suddenly, she'd be abandoned again, back to sitting on her porch and calling out to him. He's her regular.

He sits on his chair, his back bent, and stares at Nola's headstone. Then he stands and moves closer so that he can trace the letters of her name. "Hello, Nola," he says. "I'm here." He falls silent, imagining her face, imagining her in one of her aprons; that woman always did love a pretty apron. He imagines her in the kitchen turning around and saying, "What are you doing home so soon?" with great happiness. He'd come home two hours early that day, feeling ill. Just a cold, but a bad one. She'd put him to bed and then went out to get the fixings for chicken soup. While it simmered on the stove, she'd lain on the bed beside him still in her apron and asked him if he would like to talk or would he like her to read the paper to him; he hadn't had time to read it that morning. She'd laid her hand on his forehead and got up to bring him aspirin. He'd had the life of a king! She'd smelled like rose perfume and she got him anything he asked for! And he did the same for her, when she fell ill. He held her hand and stroked it. He put violets in a glass by her bed. 7UP, soda crackers. He got her whatever she needed. He left her alone when she said she wanted to be alone, which Nola mostly did when she was ill; she once said, "For God's sake, Arthur, let me *sleep!*" And so he let her sleep. But don't think he wasn't at the threshold of their bedroom checking on her every little while. Watching for the regular rise and fall of her chest.

He stands there for another minute, then goes back to sit in the chair and pull out his sandwich.

"Arthur?" he hears, and at first he thinks it's Nola and he holds stock-still, ready; he's been ready for this since the moment she died.

But it's not Nola, it's that girl, Maddy, standing a few graves away.

"Hey," she says, all somber.

"Hey," he replies, the same way, and she smiles. Sort of.

"Want some company?" she asks, and there's an edge to her voice; she's prepared for him to refuse her.

"Of course!"

She comes to sit on the ground beside him. He offers her half of his sandwich and she refuses.

"How's Nola today?" she asks.

"Still here." Arthur takes a bite of his sandwich, swallows. Again, he holds out the other half to Maddy. "You sure? It's too much for me."

She looks at it, then takes it. "Thank you."

"You're welcome."

Silence, and Arthur thinks he can feel that she's embarrassed about what she revealed when he invited her to his house, about how that lout dumped her. Arthur tried to tell her there'd be lots of other boys, but he got nowhere. Finally, they just got onto other subjects. She'd liked looking at the things in his house; she told him she liked old things, and Arthur was startled into realizing that they *were* old things, everything in his house was old. Only thing new was the food in his fridge, and even then, he'd probably do well to check the expiration dates on all the jars. Assuming he could see them. Which was doubtful. Mostly, when things smelled bad, he pitched them.

Maddy finishes her sandwich, and her mood seems lighter. When Arthur hands her a cookie, she takes it, then says around the first bite, "*Good!* What are these?"

"They're called orange blossom butter cookies."

"There's lavender in here, too." She points to a purplish fleck. "See?"

"Oh," Arthur says. "I thought that was mold."

Maddy looks up at him, taken aback. "And you *ate* them?"

"Oh, a little mold isn't going to hurt you," he says, and takes another bite.

"Where'd you buy these?" Maddy asks.

"My neighbor lady bakes all the time, and sometimes she gives me things. Lot of times, really."

"Lucky!"

"I guess I am."

She shifts to look up at him, shielding her eyes from the sun. What a pretty girl she is. If she'd just take that ring out of her nose.

"Do you have other people buried here?" she asks. "Other . . . you know, loved ones?"

"No," Arthur says. "Why do you ask?"

"I've seen you stopping at other graves."

"Ah. Yes, I stop at certain graves because . . . Well, because I seem to hear those folks. Or feel them. What I mean is, when I stand there, things about them come to me."

"You mean like a fortune-teller?"

"I don't know," Arthur says. "I've never been to a fortune-teller. But I guess it's like that. I see things like how they looked and what they wore and how they lived. Sometimes I see what they loved." He looks down at Maddy and smiles. The blood rises to his face. But Maddy seems to find nothing unusual in what he has said.

"Do you think it's really true, these . . . things you get?" she asks.

"I guess it doesn't matter, really."

She nods. "Right. What are they going to do, sue you for misrepresentation?"

The girl does have a sense of humor. He wishes she would smile more.

"It's just pleasant for me to imagine their lives," he says. "They're Nola's neighbors, I want to know who they are."

"God, you really *loved* her!" She's digging in the earth, making a little hole and filling it up, making a hole and filling it up.

"I did. I do. Always and forever. Nola Corrine."

She looks over at him. "I'm going to call you Truluv. We'll spell it T-R-U-L-U-V. That's your new name."

"And I'm going to call you Sunshine."

"Ha ha."

They sit companionably and then she says, "I really like that you want to know who's keeping Nola company. I guess you've only got me for company." Then she rushes to add, "Not all the time. Just sometimes, I mean."

Arthur feels an impulse to tell her he'd love to have her company anytime. He feels like she's the smallest little plant, dying from lack of water. But then he realizes he must tread carefully in this regard. People who don't feel cared for are not always comfortable being cared for.

A cedar waxwing offers its high-pitched trill, and Arthur points at a nearby tree. Maddy nods. "Cedar waxwing," Arthur says, and Maddy says, "I know."

He rolls up the wax paper from his lunch, stuffs it in the bag. He's still hungry, but the satisfaction he felt in having

Maddy's company was worth the price of a cookie and half a sandwich. In the fridge at home he's got half a pork chop.

He picks a blade of grass and puts it between his thumbs and makes a loud squeak.

Maddy sits up, surprised.

"How'd you do *that*?" she asks.

He picks another fat blade and shows her how to position it. "Now just blow," he says, "not too hard and not too soft."

She tries, but it doesn't work. "I can't do it," she says, and drops the blade, crosses her arms on her bent knees, and stares straight ahead.

"I couldn't do it right away, either," Arthur says. "Takes practice."

"Yeah." Then, facing him again, she says, "I feel things from the graves, too. Not specific things. But I feel something."

"What do you feel?"

"Mostly peace. Like . . . relief. Like, 'Okay, that's all, put down your pencils, even if you're not done.'"

"Put down your pencils?" Arthur asks.

"Yeah. Like what they say at the end of exams. Those exams for college."

Oh. College. Of course. She'll be off in the fall. He feels a little tinge of sorrow. "Where are you going to college?"

She snorts. "The college of I Don't Give a Fuck About College."

"You're not going?"

"No. And I don't want to talk about it."

"Fine with me," Arthur says. "Only I just want to say I don't think everyone should go to college."

She looks over at him, suspicious.

"Really? You really think that?"

"Yes, I do."

"Well, look at you. Captain Makesense."

"And look at you. Little Miss Pottymouth."

"Give me a break," Maddy says. "*Fuck* is part of the lexicon now. It's accepted."

Arthur uses a stick to draw a line around them as far as he can reach, then points to it. "See this?"

"Yeah?"

"This is the land of you and me, where such language is not accepted."

"Whoa!"

"Okay?" Arthur says.

Maddy sighs. "Yeah, fine, who gives a shit?"

He's about to chastise her again but when she smiles at him, he just can't. He smiles back and shakes his finger at her, and she laughs.

"Can I say *goldurn*?" she asks, and Arthur nods.

"*Cotton-pickin'*?"

"Say it myself," he says. "Works just as well. Don't forget about *dagnabbit*."

She leans in closer to him. "If you say *fuck* one time, I'll stop swearing. Around you."

"Really?"

She nods.

"Okay." He tries, he really does, but his throat closes. He's never used that word and he's not about to start now. "Can't do it," he tells her. "I didn't even say that when I was in the Army."

"Takes practice," Maddy says. Then she adds, "That's not even my *worst* one."

"Is that right? Well, I don't care to know the others."

"You're kind of a cool dude, Truluv," Maddy says.

And then they both sit silently until Maddy rises and says she has to go back to school. No joy in Mudville when she says that, that's for sure. He watches her walk away and a big pinch comes to his heart.

"Maddy!" he calls after her.

She turns around.

"Come over anytime. You'd be welcome anytime. Day or night. Really."

She stands there. Then, "Do I have to call first?"

"No. Come anytime. I'll be glad to see you. Gordon, too."

She puts her backpack down, takes out a pen and a note-book. "What's your address again?"

He moves closer so he doesn't have to yell it. "Three-oh-three Maple."

"Okay," she says. And maybe it's just wishful thinking, but it does seem to Arthur that her step is a bit lighter.

———

Two weeks. Two glorious weeks and Lucille has seen Frank almost every single night. On their first date, they went back to their high school, out to the bleachers where Lucille used to sit to watch Frank play football. They didn't talk much, just sat there, holding hands. Then Frank said, "I guess I've missed this place a lot," and Lucille felt the glowing hope that he would move back.

They've gone out for dinner, fancy and plain. They've gone to movies. She took him to her church and he even took communion with her. He took her to a concert, some Sinatra imitator, and she wasn't quite sure what to say. It was god-awful, of course, but Frank seemed to like it and so Lucille decided she liked it, too. Of course the guy wasn't really like Sinatra! Who could really be like Frank Sinatra but Frank Sinatra? It was just fun! It was! All the way home in his car (and if you think you don't like Cadillacs, well, you just ride in one), they sang Sinatra's song about New York.

At a stoplight, Frank had turned to her to ask, "Do you like New York City, Lucille? If you like it, I'll take you there."

Frank had done very well for himself. If they went to New York, they'd probably stay in one of those swanky hotels that had high tea in a gorgeous, high-ceilinged room, some woman wearing a formal and playing a harp while people ate tiny little sandwiches that wouldn't satisfy a pigeon, and drank tea with their pinkies sticking out.

Lucille told him the truth. "I went to New York one time with another teacher, she taught fourth grade, too. I didn't think I'd like it and I told her so. I'm not one for big cities, that's why I live here. We have quite enough going on."

"Ah yes, the teeming metropolis of Mason, Missouri," Frank said. "Population five thousand."

"Never mind, Mr. Snoot," Lucille said. "Anyway, as I was saying, my friend insisted I'd love New York. Well, we went and we walked all over and I hated it. And I said so. And she said, 'Let me show you something,' and she took me to the top of the Empire State Building. We got all the way up there on the observation deck and she said, 'Now what do you think?' And I said, 'Marge, if I hated it walking around down there, why in the world would you think I would like it up here, where all I can see are all these buildings and buildings and buildings! No,' I told her, 'I like grass. I like more space between things. I like polite people who talk slower. I like red Jell-O with fruit cocktail in there, and mayonnaise on top!'"

Frank laughed. "Well! Did that ruin the friendship?"

Lucille's face changed. "No. It didn't. We had a great friendship, she was my best friend, we could say anything to each other. She died of cancer twenty-seven years ago. I miss her still. Do you know, sometimes I still go to call her? Something happens and I think, *Wait till Marge hears this!*"

Frank looked down; he seemed sad, too. Then he stroked Lucille's cheek gently upward with the backs of his fingers and said, "Well. You see?"

She wasn't entirely sure what he meant, but she nodded.

One night, after they'd both had old-fashioneds, Frank told Lucille that he had always regretted that he hadn't married her. He'd taken her hand when he told her that, and for a moment she thought he was going to do his old move, that thrilling wrist kiss. But they were past that now, they got enough pleasure just being with each other. Oh, she takes his arm when they walk together, they share a little kiss good night, but no Frenching. No. Although maybe later. They might grow into some things. She'll see. She does dress better, and that's been fun. She went over to Chico's and got some playful prints and some jackets that hid a multitude of sins and some jewelry that was cheap but complemented the outfits nicely. "Don't you just feel younger?" the saleswoman asked, and Lucille had the oddest reaction. She wanted to say, *Listen, sister, you'll be right where I am before you know it.* She doesn't know why she had that impulse. And of course she didn't say it, she said, "Why, yes, I kind of *do* feel younger. A few years, at least."

"Seeeeee?" the woman said, and then tried to talk her into getting tank tops, but Lucille is not going there. As they say. She is *not* going there. All that stuff hanging out. No.

But here's the most wonderful thing. Frank does not seem to care about any of that. He told her that what he had always loved about her was her honesty, her openness, her simplicity, even her daffiness, it made him feel like he was Desi to her Lucy. Though when he said that, Lucille bristled. *Simplicity!* And for heaven's sake, *daffiness!* But then he explained that his wife had been so complicated, so high-maintenance, such a nag and constant complainer. Absolutely no fun. He said he was sorry to say it, it was never good to speak ill of the dead, and after all she'd been his wife for so many years. But nothing was ever right with Sue from the get-go. Nothing ever measured up, especially him. She'd accuse him of doing insensitive things and he'd have no idea what she was talking about and so she would make him sit down and she would explain it to him. In excruciating detail. Why he was such a dick, pardon the language.

"Why didn't you leave her?" Lucille asked.

He shrugged. "The same reason so many others stay in bad marriages. The children."

"Did you have affairs?" she asked.

He was silent, and she said quickly, "I'm sorry. It's not my business."

"It is your business because I want you to really know me, Lucille. I want you to know all of me. And yes, there were affairs. One was with my secretary, for twelve years."

"Twelve years!"

"Yup, she finally gave up hoping I'd leave my wife for her. Though I was clear from the start that I never would. She left and I found someone else. Odd to say it, but those affairs kept my marriage together. I couldn't leave my children."

Lucille started to feel bad, thinking, *You could have had children with me,* but then Frank said, rather shyly, "I'd really like for you to meet them, Lucille. I have a daughter and two sons, and I have four grandchildren. My grandsons are ten, fourteen, and seventeen, and my granddaughter just turned twelve. I haven't told my children about you just yet. They were utterly devoted to their mother—still are, really. She treated them a lot better than she treated me, thank goodness! But when the time is right, I'll tell them. The toughest one will be Sandy, the one who lives here. She thinks everyone is a gold digger. But she'll come around."

And Lucille said that she would love to meet them. For one thing, his daughter lived here but the boys and most of the grandchildren lived in San Diego. Perfect place to visit in the winter. And she was healthy (relatively), and Frank was healthy (relatively); they could go back and forth and really enjoy themselves.

"Do you play golf?" he'd asked her on their second date, dinner at some really good Italian restaurant (fifteen miles away!), and she'd said, "Well, sure, miniature," and he'd laughed and said good, he'd play miniature golf with her, and he hoped she would tolerate him playing nine holes every week. Just a par three course. Real flat and easy. Nobody else out there, usually; you could get through pretty quickly. He hoped she wouldn't have a problem with him playing golf once a week.

"Maybe I could try to play with you," she said, and his eyes lit up like a little boy's. "I'll bet you're a wonderful teacher." She said this a bit flirtatiously, a bit double-entendre-ly. And then he really got happy. Men were ever men, weren't they? Men were ever men. But his reaction made her feel kind of flowery and feminine.

"*God*, I'm glad I took a chance and wrote you!" he said.

"*God*, I'm glad you did, too!" Lucille said playfully, but really very seriously. She took another bite of food and then she said, "You know, Frank, when we were going out, I was always afraid to eat in front of you. I didn't want to seem unladylike. We girls used to talk about what was the best thing to eat that wouldn't make us spill or slurp or drop things off our fork. Or worst of all, get garlic on our breath!"

"I guess you wouldn't have picked spaghetti and meatballs," Frank said.

And then a little red sliver of devil came into Lucille and she made a really loud sound, slurping her pasta off the fork. *Zluuuurrrp!*

They both laughed and then Frank did it, too, and little flecks of sauce landed on his face like freckles and the other diners looked at them, which only made them laugh harder, and then Frank blew bubbles with a straw in his water.

In one more week, on June 1, she's going to ask him to move out of his daughter's house and stay with her. Not for *that*. Just so they can see how it goes, being together. Finally.

At lunchtime, Maddy leaves school and goes to the cemetery, as usual. But this time she goes to a new area; she doesn't want to run into that old man, Arthur. No. Not Arthur, *Truluv*. She doesn't want to talk to anyone, even him.

She settles herself at the base of a willow tree, where no one will see her. It's pretty here, the willow tree, a little pond off in the distance. She wonders who would ask to be buried by the pond. Actually, she would. She would like to be buried by water, so then there would be earth, air, and water all around her. Only thing missing would be fire. Maybe she could have an eternal flame, ha ha.

She takes in a deep breath. Great day, so far. She got a D on her math test and the teacher wrote at the top in red: *Maddy, you must do better!* And she has to admit it, she might as well admit it, it hurts more to deny it than to admit it: she still loves Anderson. She's not getting over him. Today, especially, her insides felt filled with ground glass. She guesses she thought he didn't mean it. She guesses she thought he'd come back. Last night she kissed her pillow like it was him because she misses kissing him so much. He was such a good kisser. Soft lips, and he used to pull at her tongue a little with his mouth, just a little sucking feeling that drove her wild. He put his finger inside her because she was still a virgin, no surprise there, who would want her? But Anderson did. They had been working up to the real thing, which Anderson said they could do once she was eighteen. One time, when they were naked, he came on her. And guess what. She treasured it. He got all panicky and said, "Wait, wait, let me wipe that off," and jumped up for his T-shirt, but she treasured it. A live part of him on her. She hates him but she misses him, and even when you hate someone you can still love them, she's proof of that.

Plus, she just had another *incident*. She's supposed to go and talk to the counselor when an *incident* occurs. Right. That'll help.

She was sitting in class and doodling, listening to Mr. Lyons talk about Langston Hughes. Nobody in class had heard of him but Maddy, and she wasn't about to raise her hand and admit it. Mr. Lyons asked if anyone had heard the simile "like a raisin in the sun." A few hands shot up fast; okay, big deal, they knew about the play. So Mr. Lyons talked about the play and then he was starting to dissect Hughes's poem "Harlem," and Maddy was interested, as she always was when they talked about poetry, it made her forget everything else, every time. But then Scott Bredeman, who sat across from her, whispered her name. She didn't look over at first, she was pretty sure no good could come of it. But he was new, he had only been there for a week, so maybe it was okay. She looked over at him and he handed her a note, put his finger to his lips, smiled at her. He had a nice smile, big dimples. He returned his attention to Mr. Lyons, and Maddy opened the note:

Your blouse is open.

She looked down. Sure enough, a button halfway down had come undone and her blouse was gaping open. Her face colored, and she quickly buttoned herself up. She stared straight ahead, listening to Mr. Lyons, but she was thinking that it was nice of Scott to tell her. He had done something nice for her.

She turned her head slightly to study him. Not only was he good-looking, he just looked like a kind person. Maybe she could have a friendship with him, and in that way start over. Maybe if he liked her, another kid would, and then another. Maybe they'd all eat lunch together eventually, and the horrible treatment she'd endured for so long would lessen, then stop. But how to start?

On the same piece of paper, she wrote, in what she hoped was a casual-looking script, *Where did you move here from?*

She passed him the note, and he read it. He thought for a moment, while her heart hammered in her chest, then wrote something and passed the note back. *Not interested, okay?*

She sat there. Sat there some more, a black ache expanding inside her. So he knew. Already, he'd been enlisted on the side of the Others. He had been told what everyone but her seems to know about her. He had also straightened his posture and moved slightly to the right in his seat, so that his back was toward her to the extent that it could be.

She looked straight ahead at all the other kids in the class. All those backs of heads holding nothing like what was in her head now, which was this: there is a scent the hounds get excited by, and the fox can't separate that scent from itself.

She slipped the note into her backpack. Couldn't leave it there. But it defiled her backpack. Her day. Her life.

When the bell rang, Mr. Lyons called over to her, "Miss Harris! Hang on for a second." And then after all the kids had filed out (Scott Bredeman looking a tiny bit worried, she was happy to see), Maddy went up to Mr. Lyons and he leaned against the edge of his desk, his arms crossed, and asked her, "What did that boy write to you?"

So he'd seen it. He saw everything.

"Nothing," she said.

Mr. Lyons waited.

"*Nothing*," Maddy said. "Just . . . the usual." She shrugged.

"Come with me," Mr. Lyons said, but Maddy said no. She knew he would bring her to the counselor or the principal. She told him she had to meet someone for lunch. Mr. Lyons said okay, doubtfully, and then he said, "Maddy, I just want you to know that it'll get better. Truly it will."

"Oh, I know," she said, and she smiled at him, which cost her. It cost her.

Now she sits under the willow tree and for the millionth time wonders why her. *Why?* She never did anything to any of them. There was an incident in sixth grade when a girl came up to her at recess and asked her if it was true her mother was dead. And when Maddy said yes, the girl's expression changed to one of guarded horror and she walked off to whisper in another girl's ear. Maddy yelled, "It's not *contagious!*" The girls made big eyes at her, then wandered off, hand in hand.

But even before that she'd been seen as weird. Not picked on in the way she is now, but weird. She supposes she is a little weird: she's quiet, certainly; she has different tastes and predilections than most people her age, but she's not like Carla Casella, who is in three of her classes. Carla wears white ankle socks every day and a little bell around her neck and she sits in the very front of every classroom and yells out answers without being called on. She chews with her mouth open so dramatically you think it's a joke and she gets a ride to and from school with a father who looks like a bigger nerd than she is. Nobody bothers Carla. They don't *include* her, but they don't bother her. Fred Kaufman carries a briefcase to school, he has a little thermos of coffee in there, he wears bow ties, he chooses to be alone rather than hang out with anyone, and everybody thinks he's the coolest thing.

Why do they pick on her?

One of the things Maddy has of her mother's is a collection of Tori Amos CDs. Maddy listens to those CDs a lot, and she's read about Tori. She draws comfort from a quote she read that was attributed to the singer: "What girls do to each other is beyond description. No Chinese torture comes close."

But of course, it's not just the girls. The boys have joined in in a way that's more desultory but every bit as constant. Every bit as determined-seeming. Maddy doesn't know what they're fixed on unless it's what someone wrote on her Facebook page before she took it down: *Die, and you'll be popular.*

Maddy has read that the inspiration for Tori Amos's song "Cornflake Girl" came from the idea of a cornflake girl as compared to a raisin girl. Raisin girls, rare, different, are much harder to find. The first line of the song is "Never was a cornflake girl . . ." Tori embraces her differentness, but Maddy doesn't have the strength Tori seems to have. Maddy wants to belong. She wants them to stop picking on her. She has thought and thought about how she might change things, she has tried to come up with solutions—funny, creative, tough, plainspoken, and sincere—but she has not been able to change anything. This amped-up abuse has been going on since junior year. She thought they'd forget about it over the summer, but they didn't forget about it; it's worse this year. Last time she went to the girls' bathroom, somebody threw a used tampon over the wall of the stall. She saw it come sailing over and then she heard some laughter and then she watched some feet walk quickly out. At least it didn't get on her. She used a big bunch of toilet paper to pick it up and tossed it in the toilet, flushed it. No point in the janitor having to do it. She came out of the stall and washed her hands and did not look at herself in the mirror and then she went to her next class. She's been off Facebook for months but they still find their ways. Last week after gym class, she went to put on her shoes and found lipstick smeared all over the soles.

Probably in every school this happens to someone. In her school, she's the one. And the winner is: *Maddy Harris!* And here's how it works: When she says her own name in her mind, she, too, feels a revulsion. They have persuaded her onto their side, though they do not let her belong with them. In this way, she does belong with them.

She walks over to a nearby grave. Anna Marie Dorset. Born 1922. Died 2000. She lies on the grave and closes her eyes. Birds sing.

She wonders what her funeral would be like, if she died now. She wonders if her father would say the eulogy. Who else would say anything? But what would her father say? What *could* he say? If he were honest, he'd say just four words: *I never knew her.*

Maddy feels something crawling up her face and sits up, brushes it away. An ant. They're amazing creatures, not everyone knows how amazing they are. They can carry fifty times their own weight.

She leans over the grave of Anna Marie. Tries to "get" something like Truluv does. But she doesn't get anything.

Here's what Maddy gets: the meaning of her favorite Langston Hughes poem, called "Suicide's Note." It's about someone understanding that something wants him, even if it's only death. It's about that person's calm acceptance of the river's request for a kiss, his feeling that now, as ever, is as good a time as any to leave.

It's time to go back. She walks slowly toward school, carrying her backpack and fifty times her own weight.

Soldier ants plug entrances to their nests so invaders can't get in. She isn't a soldier ant. Nor does she have one, anymore. "Will you come to my graduation?" she'd asked Anderson, and he'd looked pained. But then he'd said, "Yeah. Sure." And he'd kissed her like she was the cutest thing.

For the next three days, nothing but rain. Rain, thunder, lightning, the works. Arthur has stood resolutely at the bus stop every day, his umbrella pretty much useless against the sideways-blowing rain. Today when he awakens, it's still raining. *BOOM!* goes the thunder. Nola was always afraid of thunder, it sometimes even made her cry and say, "Oh, *stop!*" Gordon is afraid, too, but he won't admit it. He follows Arthur into whatever room he goes to, and if Arthur turns to look at him, he sniffs elaborately at a dust ball, at the edge of a carpet, along the bottoms of the kitchen cabinets. Or he rolls on his back and stares at Arthur through green slits.

Today Arthur would like to stay in all day and listen to his

Dinah Shore tapes, but a man has to do what a man has to do. When he thinks of the harsh winter days he spent beside Nola's grave when the wind seemed like it was going to yank the trees right out of the ground and the cold reddened his cheeks and nose, rain seems like nothing.

But by the time Arthur showers, dresses, and eats a breakfast of an English muffin with sardines (definitely not the taste he was hoping for), the rain has finally stopped. The sun has come out in a way that seems indifferent, defensive, as if nothing at all has happened in its absence. Puddles are still deep enough for ducks, and all the branches that fell haven't been cleared away, but the sky is clear.

He spends a longer time than usual at the cemetery—he falls asleep, if the truth be told, but even in sleep he has Nola on his mind. He's stiff in the shoulders and the knees and the neck when he walks to the bus stop to go home; he hopes a hot shower will help.

When he comes up onto his porch, he sees a small cardboard box at the door. Inside are five cans of that fancy cat food in ads where the cat eats out of a crystal goblet with a tiara on its head. There's also a piece of paper, folded over, *Truluv* written on it in a backhand script, purple ink.

He looks inside the note. There's a photo of Gordon, looking as handsome as can be, looking like King Tut, especially since she has Photoshopped a crown on his head. What the kids can't do with those computers! He's seen what look like four-year-olds seated at little computer screens at the library, intent on their business as air traffic controllers.

So Maddy was here! But when did she take that photo? When she was at his house, he didn't see her take any photos. Such a wonderfully strange girl.

Beneath Gordon's image, she has written: *Maybe I'll see you at the cemetery tomorrow. It will be my birthday.*

She'll be eighteen, he remembers. He'll bring her a present. Something special.

"Gordon?" he calls, when he lets himself inside. "Gordon!" No sign of him. "*Gordon!*"

The hell with him. Arthur sets the box down and then sees the cat, just off to the side, not one foot away, staring at him.

"You couldn't walk over?" Arthur says. "You couldn't take two steps?"

Gordon blinks.

Arthur points to the box. "You know what's in there? You won't *believe* what's in there." His chest seizes up suddenly and he begins coughing so spectacularly that Gordon runs away. Arthur makes his way upstairs, coughing all the while. Yes, a hot shower, that's what he needs. Pronto.

Arthur's shower is brief, but he thinks maybe it helped. He puts on his pajamas, even if it is only five o'clock, and comes downstairs to open up a can of something for dinner. He thinks he has some of that O spaghetti; it's not too bad if you add a lot of cheese. He's got a hot dog or two. An apple.

He opens the drawer for the can opener and sees Mr. and Mrs. Hamburger. "Bingo," he says. "Happy birthday to you."

Somewhere in the house, there's wrapping paper. Nola always said half the gift was the wrapping, and she knocked herself out in that regard. Once she wrapped a coat for her mother and Arthur told her the gift looked like an entry for the Macy's Thanksgiving Day Parade.

"I'll take that as a compliment," Nola said, and he said, "I meant it as one!" Though that wasn't precisely true.

He thinks maybe the wrapping paper is in the back of her closet. He thinks he remembers her always going there to get it.

He washes off the figures with a little Comet cleanser until they look almost new. Nothing he can do about the way the rubber has yellowed, but at least there are no crumbs stuck in the corners of their smiles, or in the latch of Mrs. Hamburger's purse.

He heads upstairs for the wrapping paper and suddenly stops. He clutches at the railing with one hand, at his chest with the other, and then he lowers himself down on the step to catch his breath. Well, that's new. And here comes Gordon, who likes nothing more than to gaze impassively upon another's suffering, that of mice or men. He smiles at his own joke. He'll have to tell Maddy that one. He scratches the top of the cat's head, and Gordon closes his eyes and stretches his neck up at an improbable angle in pleasure. If Arthur came upon the cat lying on the floor that way, he'd think Gordon had broken his neck. People think cats aren't entertaining, but they are.

After a moment, Arthur gets up again and goes into Nola's closet, which he has yet to empty and why should he, he doesn't think he will ever remove a single thing from there, not the dresses, not the skirts or blouses, not the scarves or the hats or the shoes or the purses. Not the little beaded black coin purse she used when her back was bothering her too much to carry a regular purse. On the right kind of day, he can still smell her in that closet.

He sees that he was right, there in the back of the closet are plastic bins holding wrapping paper and ribbon. He finds a package of paper with lilacs on it, big bouquets of lilacs, and there's some purple ribbon wrapped up right with the paper. Couldn't be easier! He brings the supplies downstairs and wraps the figurines, and then has to sit at the kitchen table to catch his breath again. He's disappointed at the way the gift looks, all lumpy and bumpy and the tape showing; Nola would never let the tape show, but he has no idea how to do that. The ribbon is pretty but the bow is nothing elaborate. Maybe he'll tape a purple rose on it tomorrow before he takes it over to the cemetery. He grows a variety called Amnesia, maybe it'll help Maddy forget her troubles. He also has a darker purple one called Moody Blue, she might like that one even better. After dinner, he'll make her a card and sign it, *Your friends, Truluv and Gordon.*

But then he decides to skip dinner. He's not hungry. What he is is exhausted. He makes his way back upstairs, then realizes he hasn't fed Gordon. And so he comes back down. And then goes back up. He'll tell Maddy that Gordon devoured that cat food. That's what he'll tell her, though what happened is that the cat sniffed it and then walked away from it. Sat expectantly a distance away as if he were saying, *What else you got?* Well, the cat had to get fed. He had to eat. Arthur gave him a hot dog. He couldn't get mad at him. They were alike, he and Gordon. Fancy food didn't impress them.

Arthur falls asleep instantly, and he has a dream. He dreams that it is summer and he is out in the front yard deadheading the roses and he becomes aware of something behind him. When he turns around, there is Nola, standing on the sidewalk in front of their house. She is young again, and beautiful, and her face is flushed with pleasure the way it used to get.

"Nola?" he says, his heart in his throat.

She smiles.

He walks a few steps closer. "Are you . . . Can I touch you?"

She nods. He drops the clippers and moves slowly toward her. When he is right in front of her, he sees the dampness in her eyes, he hears the breath moving in and out of her, he smells her perfume and sees the gentle wind moving her hair and he cries out and embraces her. He says her name over and over, he tells her he misses her so much, he kisses her neck, her shoulder, and then he pulls back away to look into her eyes. She says nothing.

"Can you talk?" he asks, tears wet on his face.

She shakes her head no.

"That's all right," he says. And then, "Would you like to sit on the porch with me?"

She nods, and they hold hands and walk up the steps together like they did so many times, so many times — as young people, as middle-aged people, as old people. He sits on his chair and waits for her to sit on hers. But she doesn't sit there, she sits on his lap, oh, he can feel warmth and her weight, she is real and she has come back to him. She smiles into his face and then leans over to slip off her shoes, she always did like to slip off her shoes in the warm weather. And then, even though she is so young and beautiful and he is an old man with patches of white whiskers he misses with the razor, with cloudy eyes and aching joints, with a turkey neck and a concave chest and a shuffling gait, she kisses him full on the mouth for a long, long time. Her hand rests lightly against the side of his face. Her breasts are pressing into him. He is about to lead her upstairs when he awakens.

The room is gray; dawn has come. "No," Arthur says. "Go back to sleep."

He closes his eyes, thinks of Nola's clove-scented breath, her bare feet, the little white buttons down the front of her dress. *Come back, come back!* He has heard that people can wake up from dreams and then will themselves right back into them. But not him, apparently. She is gone. Again.

He turns over and shoves his face into his pillow and weeps, a horrible, hoarse, creaky-gate sound, an old-man sound. A man-utterly-alone sound.

He can't go to the cemetery today. He can't see her headstone, he can't see the earth packed over her coffin. Her down there all alone in the darkness. He won't go there. He will spend the whole day trying to dream her back to him. And anyway, he feels lousy. Sometime in the night, when he got up to pee, he brought up a bunch of crap from his lungs.

His neck hurts. His legs. His arms. His heart. His soul. His bedroom and his clothes and the glasses in the kitchen cupboard, they hurt.

He goes downstairs to feed Gordon another hot dog and to empty his litter box. In another bowl he puts a big pile of dry cat food, which the cat disdains, he only likes it when it's given in small amounts, but Arthur's not sure he can make it downstairs again. Not today.

When he starts back up to his bedroom he hears Gordon meow. "No," he says. "I can't."

Maddy waits at Nola's grave for her entire lunch period. The old man doesn't show.

When it's time to go back to school, she goes back. A couple of weeks until graduation and done.

Her father brings home frozen enchiladas for her birthday dinner and they eat them on plates rather than out of the microwave containers. He also got two huge cupcakes from the bakery, and after the enchiladas he puts a candle in hers and she obligingly blows it out while he sings two lines of the Happy Birthday song. Then he hands her a card, a musical one, the Beatles singing, *You say it's your birthday!* Inside are two brand-new one-hundred-dollar bills. She looks up at her father and he says, "Happy birthday."

"It's too much," she says, and he says, again, "Happy birthday."

Later, when she's doing calculus homework in her bed-

room, her father knocks at the door, tells her he's going grocery shopping, does she need anything? She wants to leap
up from her desk and scream, *Do I NEED anything? Do I
NEED ANYTHING? Are you fucking BLIND?*

What she does say is "Frosted Mini-Wheats? Blueberry
kind?"

"Okay," her father says, entering it into his phone. "Anything else? Any . . . feminine things?" He keeps his eyes focused on the phone.

"Tampax, pearl, regular," she says, and he dutifully en-
ters it.

But she doesn't need Tampax. And at this moment, she
understands why. She understands why her boobs hurt, why
she's had weird episodes of nausea. And now she sits calmly
before her father with her brain all pinbally and she doesn't
know what to do. What should she do? And then she thinks,
I'll call Anderson. This is no tragedy. This is a get-out-of-jail-
free card.

"I'll be back," her father says.

"Okay."

Maddy cleans up the kitchen, then goes back to her
room and gets her phone, lies on her bed, and takes in a
deep breath.

It could work. He really liked her at first. *Really* liked her.
He may be a jerk at times, but he's responsible, he is up for
assistant manager. And he likes kids, he loves them, as does
she; he told her that once, he said he wanted a lot of kids.
She asked him how many and he said one hundred. All girls
that look like you, he said.

A baby is so cute, how can you not love a baby? She won't be sad around Anderson anymore. She won't be weird. Everything will be solid, this will bring them together, they will be a family, she will have a family like other people have.

Maddy taps his name on her phone. He picks up, that's the first good thing.

"Hey, Maddy." His voice is warm. Second good thing.

"How are you?" he asks. Jackpot, he wants to talk.

"I'm good!" she says. "How about you?"

"All right," he says. "I kind of miss you, kid."

"I miss you, too." She wants to cry but she knows better. Keep it light. He always likes to keep it light.

"Hey, I had a birthday!" she says.

"When?"

"It's . . . today, actually."

"Happy birthday! So you're eighteen, right?"

"Right!"

"What'd you get?"

"You mean . . . ? Oh, I got a card. And some money. From my dad."

Anderson snorts. He doesn't think much of her dad.

"It was nice, I can buy some clothes or something. Some books."

"Yeah, you like your books, don't you?"

She reaches down to hold tightly on to her ankle. "So . . . are you still with that woman you work with?"

"I don't know. More or less."

He's bored with her, Maddy thinks. Already.

"Would you ever want to . . . get together?" she asks.

He doesn't answer. She bites her lip, waits.

Finally, he laughs.

"I just meant—"

"What are you doing tonight?"

She sits up, triumphant. But then, "Well, it's a school night," she says. Her dad is an idiot about that stuff.

"You could sneak out again."

She supposes she could. But wait, then she would tell him face-to-face. What if he got mad?

"Come on," he says. "We'll have a do-over. A do-over *plus*."

She looks out the window, where the streetlights have just come on.

"Anderson, I have to tell you something."

"What?"

"I seem to be pregnant."

Silence. Then, "What are you talking about?"

"I haven't done the test. But I'm late." The word feels sideways in her mouth.

"Well, you can't be pregnant. Not from me. I never even came in you."

"No, but remember that time you came *on* me kind of . . . low?"

"*Fuck!*"

She stops breathing, says nothing. Presses the phone closer to her ear.

"Listen, Maddy, you're not going to pin this on me.

You're not going to trap me. I didn't do anything. I don't know why you're even telling me this. What do you expect me to do about it?"

She closes her eyes, rocks back and forth. "I thought . . ."

"You thought what? Oh, Christ, you didn't think I'd like *marry* you or some shit, did you?"

"No, no, not that, but maybe I could live with you. I could take care of you. We used to have a good time. You like kids; you're good with kids, you told me you want to have a lot of kids."

"You're crazy, Maddy. You really are. I mean bona fide. You're fucking crazy, okay? You need help. Get some help. And take that money your dad gave you and get yourself an abortion. I want nothing to do with this. It isn't even mine. Don't call me anymore. Get some help, Maddy, I'm not kidding."

He hangs up.

She sits unmoving until she hears her father's car pull up. And then she hears him calling her.

She goes out into the kitchen. "What."

"Nice greeting!"

"Sorry."

He takes the shredded wheat from a bag. "Here's your cereal."

"Thanks."

"Put it away, will you?"

She puts it on the cereal shelf, then silently helps to put away the other groceries.

"So I've been thinking about graduation," her father says.

"We'd better make a reservation for dinner after the ceremony. Where would you like to go?"

"Nowhere," she says, and her father says, "Nice."

"I don't mean it like that," she says. "I just . . . I don't like my school. You know that. I don't like the kids there. I don't fit in."

"Oh, every teenager feels that way," her father says. "I felt that way myself."

"No, they're mean to me, you know?" Her voice is shaky; she is close to tears.

"Why are they *mean?*" her father asks. "What do they do?"

She stands there. Then, "Never mind," she says. She starts to walk away, and her father takes her arm. "Well, *tell* me. What do they do?"

She doesn't answer, and her father sighs. "You've got to toughen up, Maddy. It's a rough world out there."

"Right."

"Sometimes you just have to let things roll off your back."

"Yeah. Like you do, Dad?"

He stares at her for a long time. Then he says, "That's different. I hope someday you can understand."

"I hope so, too. In the meantime, can I skip graduation?"

"You're going to graduation. For God's sake, Maddy, do you always have to be so melodramatic?"

"I'm not going," she says. "We don't have to go. And I'm not. I'm *not going!*" Her voice echoes in the room, she's almost screaming.

Her father holds up his hands. "*Fine!*" he says. "Get a

refund on the cap and gown. I suppose you don't want to go out to a restaurant, either."

"What would be the point, Dad?"

"To celebrate? I'm proud of you?"

She laughs.

"Maddy, I don't know what to say to you. I have never known what to say to you. I just . . . I can't . . ."

Is he going to *cry*? She looks into his face, touches his arm. "It's okay," she says.

He shakes his head. "Oh, Christ, Maddy. It's your birthday."

"Yeah. So I guess I'd like to take a walk, okay?"

He starts to put his jacket on.

"Alone," she says. "No offense."

"Okay," he says. "Okay."

She walks to the drugstore a mile away. She buys a pregnancy test and goes into the bathroom to use it. When she comes out, she buys a sippy cup. A rattle. A yellow washcloth with a duck on it. And a little stuffed bear that is 60 percent off because his ribbon is stained.

She's keeping this baby. It is hers. And in it, and through it, she will remake the world. She, too, will get born, into another kind of life.

On June 1, the first day of the month for weddings, Lucille closes the door behind her and Frank, then locks it. She turns around and says softly, "Well, Mr. Snow, here I am."

Frank looks confused.

"*Carousel?*" Lucille says. "That song in the play *Carousel?*"

"Never saw it," Frank says, embarrassed-looking, and Lucille thinks it's the sweetest thing.

"Not even the movie?" she asks, and he says no.

"Well," she says. "I'll get it out of the library and we'll watch it. And we'll have a clambake after we watch it, there's a clambake in there. Or, you know, we'll go out to Red Lobster."

"I like Red Lobster," Frank says.

"Me, too."

"I like the Create Your Own combination."

"Me, too!"

Frank clears his throat and sticks his hands in his pockets. Then, "Are we stalling?"

Lucille nods. "I guess so."

"Let's go upstairs. Shall I carry you?"

"Very funny," says Lucille, and Frank says, "It's the thought that counts."

When they reach her bedroom, Frank sits at the edge of her bed and Lucille pulls down the shades. Then she comes to stand before him.

"I don't know what to do," she says.

He pats the bed beside him. "Just come sit."

She does, and they sit staring straight ahead. Then he reaches over to take her hand like it's a Fabergé egg.

Lucille begins to cry, unexpectedly. It's embarrassing to her; she wipes her eyes quickly, then laughs.

"It's okay," Frank says. "It's been a long time." He takes off his glasses and lays them carefully on the nightstand. Lucille takes off her glasses, too. And then she does something astonishing: she whips her wig off her head, exposing her thin, thin hair that you can see her scalp through, plain as day.

Frank stares at her.

"There!" Lucille says. "You might as well know!"

She kneads the wig she's holding in her lap, then tosses it on top of their glasses.

"Lucille, I already knew," Frank says softly.

"What?"

"I say I already *knew*. That you wear a wig."

"You did?"

"Yeah. I did."

"How did you know?"

"It's . . . you know, it's a bit crooked, sweetheart."

"It *is*?" But she's been going around like this! Everywhere!

Well, at least he told her. Now she knows. At least he isn't like Ben Stoltz, the man she ate with at the last church social, who smiled at her sort of funny the whole time and then when she got home there was a big piece of spinach stuck between her front teeth.

Lucille turns to face Frank fully. "I appreciate your honesty, Frank. I think we should always be honest with each other."

"Do you?"

"Yes, I do."

He nods, staring into his lap. "Okay. Well, then I think I should tell you I had prostate cancer. I'm fine now, but . . . you know."

"Oh, my. Were you scared when you got diagnosed?"

He looks over at her. "I guess so. I guess I was scared. But mostly, I just wanted to keep on living. I mean, after I turned fifty, I realized that things were going to start *happening,* you know? I lost a buddy to cancer when he was only thirty-seven. I was lucky I lived so long without anything happening to me. I was seventy-nine when I was diagnosed. And you know, I wasn't even surprised. I thought, *Huh. So this is what's going to take me out.* It didn't, of course, all it did was wake me up a little. And remind me that other things are going to happen."

Lucille nods. "Some of the things that happen when we get older are good, though."

"Some of the things are very good. And surprising. And some things are so . . ." He stops, turns to her, and she sees that his eyes are wet. "Lucille. I still love you. I never stopped."

"Oh, Frank," she says. "You're my dream come true. Honestly."

They lie down and kiss a little and then it's as though they both run out of gas. But it's nice, it's very nice, they're comfortably out of gas together.

"Would you like to stay here tonight?" Lucille asks.

"Well, I don't have my things."

"What do you need?"

"Oh, you know, pajamas, for starters."

"You can wear one of my nighties," Lucille says, and starts giggling.

"Wait a minute," Frank says. "Is this one of those reality shows?"

And then they lie quietly and the night deepens around them. After a while, Lucille sits up at the side of the bed to take off her clothes, and on the other side of the bed, Frank does the same. Then they lie down and face each other, Lucille holding the sheet up high, to just beneath her chin. Frank tugs gently at the sheet and says, "You don't have to do that."

"Oh yes I do. And don't you dare look."

"At what?" he asks, smiling.

She clamps her lips tightly together and then says, "At my sacky old breasts. And my big fat belly, and my . . . Well, I don't even know what they are. My brown spots."

"Lucille, I hope you don't mind my asking, but do you have anything really wrong with you that I should know about?"

"Oh, high cholesterol. High blood pressure. Treated with medication. A little skin cancer here and there, but who doesn't have that? Even dogs get that. But otherwise, I never even had surgery. I still have my wisdom teeth. And my appendix. And my tonsils!"

"Ohhhhh," says Frank. "I think I'm getting aroused."

Lucille's eyes widen.

"I'm kidding!" he says. "I can't, Lucille. I had a prostatectomy, and I can't. And I might as well dump the rest on you: I have to get a carotid endarterectomy."

"When?"

"I don't know, soon. I keep putting it off."

Lucille puts her head on his chest. "Oh, my beautiful wounded Frank."

He kisses the top of her head. "Oh, my long-lost Lucille. Found."

Lucille turns out the light, tenderly. But then she whispers, "Frank?"

"Yes?"

"I hope we get to be together for a long time."

"So do I."

"And I hope we get to be together in heaven, too." She doesn't want to say that that damn Sue might try to interfere. Again. But this time, he'll push her away in a nice, heavenly way. "No thanks," he'll say. "I've got what I always wanted."

Frank says, "You know, Lucille, when I was a little kid, I used to try to imagine heaven, and it just seemed boring to me. The idea of living forever, it seemed *boring*. I preferred the way things happened here. Beginnings and endings. Starts and finishes. Risks. Uncertainties. I even liked the mysteries, the ever-unknowns. I mean, we don't know where we come from, really; and when we die, we don't know where we go."

"*Heaven*," Lucille insists. "Or, you know, pitchfork city."

"Well, that's what a lot of people say. But we don't *know*. My way of looking at it is, who cares what happens before we're born and after we die? The question that has become increasingly important to me is, what do we do in the meantime?"

"That's my question, too," Lucille says. "Now."

Frank leans up on one elbow to look down at her. His eyes are still so pretty. Royal blue. "I just want you to know that I only asked if you had anything wrong because I was curious. Nothing would drive me away again, unless it was you telling me to get lost."

"I'm not going to do that. I'm going to ask you to move in with me."

He smiles. "Really?"

"Really."

"Okay." He lies back down. "Okay then."

They sleep spoons. That's all they do. After a while, he snores, a very polite snore, she thinks. She is so happy it hurts a little.

"Aw, Jesus, Maddy," her father says, rubbing his forehead. "Are you sure?" They have just finished dinner; the dishes aren't even cleared. Maddy's napkin is still in her lap.

"Yes," she says. "I did the test. Twice."

"But have you gone to a medical clinic?"

"No."

"How far along are you?"

"Almost three months, I think."

"All right." He looks at his watch, pushes back from the table, and stands. "Let's go."

"Go where?" The absurd thought comes to her that she has a lot of homework, she can't go anywhere. Ordinarily, she wouldn't care, but she's behind in Mr. Lyons's class, and she doesn't want to disappoint him. She's got almost a hundred pages of reading to do, then a paper to write. She will not disappoint him.

"To an urgent-care clinic. They're open twenty-four hours, and you can just walk in. There's one out on 45, in Nolan. Let's make sure you're pregnant, and then . . . and then we'll see."

"There's one right here. We don't have to go all the way to Nolan."

"We're going to Nolan."

"But the one right here is the same—"

"I said we're going to Nolan!"

Oh, Maddy thinks. *He's ashamed.* She doesn't blame him.

"I can't go now," she says. "I have too much homework."

Her father turns around. "Well, that's rich. I'd say if you'd been doing your 'homework,' you wouldn't have gotten yourself in this situation, would you? I cannot believe you were so stupid. Who's the father, anyway?"

She swallows. "I don't know." She won't have him contacting Anderson. She won't.

Her father's face drains of any feeling she might read. "Get in the car. Right now."

"Dad."

"What, Maddy? *What?* What do you want me to do? We've got to take care of this! Now! Every day that goes by that thing gets bigger!"

That thing.

"But I . . . I might want to keep it."

"*What?*"

She looks up at him. "I want to keep it."

"You're not keeping it. You are not keeping it. You are not going to ruin your life by having a baby at eighteen. No."

"You can't make me have an *abortion*, Dad."

"I can and I will."

"I'm eighteen."

"You know nothing! Get in the goddamn car, Maddy."

She sits there. Then she says, "I have to get my purse."

"I'll be in the car."

Maddy goes in her room, packs up her English home-work, leaves the rest of her books, and grabs her purse. She goes quietly out the back door and crosses the neighbor's lawn until she is on the next street over. Then she walks toward the little strip mall where the bus stops.

She's almost there when she hears a car honking. It's her father, and, seeing her, he pulls over, leaps out, and runs to grab her arm before she can even think about running. His grip is tight, he's hurting her, and she tells him so. He doesn't react at all, just keeps pulling her toward the car. He's breath-ing fast; his face is red; she's never seen him this way. She drops her book, the book for Mr. Lyons, and he keeps pulling.

"Wait," she says. "I dropped my book!"

He ignores her, and she wrenches free from him to go back. She grabs the book and then stands unmoving in the middle of the road, weeping.

He comes to stand beside her and speaks in a low voice from between clenched teeth. "Stop it! Get in the car."

"I'm going!"

Once she's seated, she stops crying, but oh, it hurts in her heart more than it ever has. There is a buzz saw turning round and round in there. There is a fire. There is something falling, like a pendulum on a long, long string has been cut loose. Something rubs against something else. Something bleeds. She looks out the window. It grows. It grows. She looks at her knees. It grows. She buries her nails deep into her upper arms, and, with the shock of this pain, the other pain lessens somewhat. That still works. She digs her nails in deeper until she can breathe.

"Dad—"

"I don't want to talk now. We'll talk at home."

They drive home and go into the house, but they do not talk there, either. Instead, her father sends her to her room. She sits there for a while, then begins to read the book for Mr. Lyons. Royal Lyons: *It'll get better.*

She closes the book, her finger marking the place, and tells herself, *Decide.* And just like that, she does.

The door opens and her father sticks his head in. "Tomorrow at nine A.M., I'm taking you in."

"I have school."

"Nine."

"I'm not going, Dad. I'm sorry, but I'm having the baby and I'm going to keep it."

"The appointment is not for an abortion, Maddy. The appointment is for an exam."

An exam, after which he'll make her make another appointment to get *that thing* out of there. "I'll make my own appointment."

"You have no idea how to handle this, Maddy! And you will go with me tomorrow."

"I will not."

He comes to stand before her and shakes his head. When he speaks, his voice is hoarse. "She died for this? For this life you're living? You're killing her twice."

He walks out of her room, slamming the door behind him. She hears him leave the house, slamming that door, too, and then there is the sound of his car, driving away.

She sits hunched over, her eyes wide and staring. *Hey, we have a new first name for you, wanna hear it?* She didn't answer. A group of girls, Krissi Berman and her squad. *Hey, better listen to your new name. It's Saddy. Do you like it?*

She goes to the window to look out at the wind moving the tops of the trees. First forward, then back, then side to side, as though they're following orders. And then still. Then perfectly still. She presses her forehead against the glass. Closes her eyes. They're right. She is sad. Always. Even in joy, a downward pull will come: *Don't forget.*

She could go into the bathroom and fill the tub. Slice both wrists up and down, not across. It wouldn't take that long. It wouldn't hurt that much.

She goes into the bathroom and closes the door behind her. Stares at the tub. Then she goes back into her room and finds the book she is going to read for Mr. Lyons. She feels as though a hand has come to rest on her shoulder. *Look for the helpers.*

If it had been her mother she'd told she was pregnant. If her mother had been there and listened, then nodded and said, "Let's talk about what our options are here." If, that night, before Maddy went to sleep, her mother had come to sit at the side of her bed and kissed her forehead and pushed her hair back from her face and said, "I know it seems impossible now. But things have a way of working out. I'm here and I love you."

She feels the hand move from her shoulder, and an arm come around her. A squeeze. And then: gone.

Maddy reads like a man rescued from the desert drinks a glass of water. She puts her own hand on her shoulder.

Robert Emmet Kelly. Born on Valentine's Day in 1953. Died June 14, 2015. Sixty-two. Too young! Newish grave, really; the man is still settling in. Still, Arthur steps closer and closes his eyes. *A problem with weight all his life, he told people he was even a fat baby, and he was. Liked to put sauerkraut on every meat sandwich he made. The right song could make him cry and cry. A football star, yet still not that popular with the girls. Liked model trains, had an elaborate layout in a basement where there was a constant drip he never did fix.*

That's all. It's enough, though. He doesn't need any— Wait. *He got a red robe for Christmas one year and put it right on, stepped back for a photo, and it caught on fire.* Caught on fire? From what? *A candle burning on the coffee table caught the hem. He whipped the robe off and stomped on it, put the fire out. Everyone had been hollering bloody*

murder, but Bob held up his hand and said very calmly, "It's
out, Merry Christmas, let's eat," and everyone laughed.

Arthur looks around for Maddy. No sign of her. He hasn't
seen her for . . . a week? Longer. After skipping that one day,
Arthur has come out to the cemetery every day and he has
not seen Maddy one time. Yesterday, he went to the library
and got some help on the computer to try that Facebook, to
see if he could find her there. Nope. "Have you tried Twitter?" the librarian asked. "Instagram? Snapchat?" Arthur
stared at her, then thanked her and went home to lie down.
Libraries used to be sanctuaries. Quiet places, with shafts of
sunlight falling on rows and rows of books. Stories seeming
to beckon. Now there is too much to do there, too much to
see. He doesn't do well with such stimulation. He's more of
a one-thing-at-a-time man.

A breeze rises up and Arthur shivers. His cold is better,
though he still feels punk. But he had to see Nola and he
hoped he'd see Maddy. He's brought her birthday gift every
day, and the wrapping is beginning to look a little tatty. A
hole in one corner. He supposes he should rewrap it, but he
hasn't yet.

He opens his chair at the foot of Nola's grave, puts the
present down, and takes his sandwich out of the bread bag
he used for a lunchbox. Baloney and mustard, you can't
beat that. Some potato chips. A big fat dill pickle. A little
box of apple juice. And some molasses cookies that Lucille
gave him that practically lift him up in the air, they're so
delicious, and he told her so. She accepted the compliment
with an outsize gaiety. She's almost reeling, she's so happy

lately. Something's going on, but she hasn't told him what yet.

Arthur takes a bite of his sandwich and looks around. No one is out here today, so far as he can see. Once again he is alone, yet feeling that he is in good company.

He leans over to pat Nola's headstone. "I miss you," he says. "I still miss you, sweetheart. Every day is like the first day I lost you. Now don't feel bad, I get by, you can see I get by. You've seen my new friend, Maddy. She's got that ring in her nose, but she's a nice kid. Lucille and I are getting friendly. And I take care of things. I make it through. I even whistle sometimes, but, Nola, I miss you so much. We used to talk about who would go first, and I always wished it would be me." He takes another bite of his sandwich.

After he has eaten and is about ready to leave, he stands and takes one last look around the cemetery. "Maddy?" he calls, toward a distant line of trees. He turns to face the opposite direction. "*Maddy?*" Then he stops. Shouldn't be yelling in a cemetery.

Well, the kid's lost interest. Not so unusual. He won't be giving her a birthday gift after all. He hopes she had a nice birthday. He's guessing it was a quiet one.

"Hey, Nola," he says suddenly. "I brought you a present." Of course she'll know he brought it for Maddy, she knows everything now. But she won't mind. She was ever generous-hearted, was Nola Corrine.

He unwraps Mr. and Mrs. Hamburger and rests it at the base of Nola's headstone. It looks good there. It looks absurd, but it looks good. "Remember?" he says, and then an awful load of sorrow comes to sit on his chest. He folds up his chair and walks slowly to the bus stop. No Nola. No Maddy. At least there's that ingrate Gordon. And Lucille. He might ask her to dinner again. They didn't have such a bad time, last time. Couple of laughs. And a bit of comfort. He'd confessed that the other day he couldn't find his wallet and then he found it in the refrigerator. She'd said, "Oh, pooh, I do that kind of thing all the time. Last week I found my rolling pin in the laundry hamper." It made him feel better.

He coughs, coughs, coughs, all the way to the bus stop. He's going to have to go to see that robber, Dr. Greenbaum. Get some antibiotics. Something. Sometimes Arthur forgets how old he is. Sometimes he remembers all too well.

When Arthur is walking down his sidewalk, almost home, he sees Lucille climbing up her front steps. "Lucille!" he calls out.

She turns around expectantly and he realizes he has nothing to say. When he gets up to her, he says, "Well!"

"Hello, Arthur," she says. The keys are in her hand. She wants to go inside.

But he wants some company and so he says, "What have you been up to?"

She looks at him in a kind of sideways way, as though considering something. Then she says, "Come and sit with me. I'll tell you."

Arthur comes onto the porch and settles himself into what he thinks of as his chair. Lucille sits beside him and smiles.

"You look different," he tells her.

"Well, I stopped wearing my wig. Did you know I used to wear a wig?"

He's not sure how to answer and so he makes a kind of grunting sound that could mean yes or no.

"I used to wear a wig but someone talked me out of it. 'You don't need a wig!' he said. 'It's no sin to have thinning hair!' And you know what? He's right. So I have gone natural. And I lost a little weight."

"Are you okay?"

"Yes! I wanted to lose some."

"Oh." He feels something else is required here, so he says, "Well, you look good."

"Thank you. Did you go and visit Nola today?"

"I did."

She sighs. "I suppose it brings you comfort."

"It does." He stares out at the Miss Kim lilacs that grow in front of Lucille's house. That scent! Every spring, Nola used to fill the house with lilacs from their tree in the back-yard. Even the bathroom had a bouquet. Even the laundry room. She would sprinkle blossoms in her hair, she would make a pin out of a sprig of lilac and put it on her dress. Her favorite flower.

He tells Lucille, "I loved Nola an awful lot."

"I know you did, Arthur."

"You never really knew her."

"You kept to yourselves, you two."

"We did. I'm sorry."

"Nothing to apologize for. I know the feeling. I know the

feeling now, because I have reconnected with my old boyfriend from high school."

"Really!" Arthur sneezes, then apologizes. "Getting me all excited here," he says.

"Yes, his name is Frank Pearson and he's the loveliest man. He was the loveliest boy and now he's the loveliest man."

"He lives here?"

"No, he lives in San Diego. He came here after he wrote me a letter and . . . Oh, all right, I'll just tell you, Arthur, that I am in love. Isn't it something? Maybe it's foolish. But I'm in love. We both are. With each other."

"I don't think it's foolish. I don't think love is ever foolish."

"Well, but you and I are old-fashioned." She starts to move back and forth in her chair. "Look at us old people, out here in our rocking chairs."

Arthur starts rocking, too. "I suppose we might be old-fashioned, but I don't think love is. Who doesn't need it? We all of us need it, especially those who say they don't. It's like oil in the crankcase, we can't run without it."

Quiet, and then Lucille asks, "What *is* a crankcase, anyway?"

Arthur thinks for a minute, then says, "I don't know. I have no idea. If I were a young man, I would probably make something up. But now that I'm old, well, I will just flat-out say I don't know. That, or I don't remember. Either way, I don't really care."

"Might as well be honest, at this point in our lives," Lucille says.

Arthur nods. "No time to waste on pretending."

THE STORY OF ARTHUR TRULUV 101

"That's right. No time to waste. And that's why I asked Frank to move in with me."

Arthur turns around to look at Lucille's door. "He's in there?"

"No, not now. He's at his daughter's house, giving her the news. He didn't want me to be there. I don't think it's going to go well. He told me that his daughter is a real pill."

"He called his daughter a pill?"

Lucille shrugs. "Not in so many words. But it's what he meant. I'm going to pick him up later. Say, would you like to meet him? Would you like to have dinner with us tonight?"

"I surely would," Arthur says. "Thank you."

"Six o'clock," Lucille says. And then she shows Arthur her left hand. At first he thinks she's showing him that it's shaking and he's all set to reassure her and tell her that sometimes his hand shakes, too, but it's not that. What she's showing him is a ring on her pinkie. Tiny little diamond winking in the light.

"Engagement ring?" Arthur asks.

Lucille nods.

"Well, congratulations!" He wonders if she's the oldest bride ever. But no, he's read about matches made in nursing homes between people so old they look like apple dolls. But *happy* apple dolls. No, love is never foolish. Or unnecessary.

"Beautiful ring," Arthur says. Nola taught him that. *Always* say an engagement ring is beautiful. Because it always is.

"Thank you. Do you know, he bought this for me when

we were seniors in high school? He took all his money from his summer jobs to buy it and he was going to propose on graduation day. But then . . . Well, he ended up marrying someone else. He had to. But he kept this ring all these years—imagine!—and last night he gave it to me." She looks down upon it with a blushing tenderness. "We'll have to get it sized, of course, my finger is way bigger than it used to be. But I'm wearing it anyway!"

"'Course you are!"

She stands. "Well, I've got to go in, Arthur. I'm making a fancy dessert that requires some refrigeration time." She unlocks the door, says over her shoulder, "I'll see you for dinner."

He hesitates. "Should I . . . dress?"

She laughs. "Well, don't come naked!"

"I just meant—"

"I know. Just be comfortable, Arthur. I'll see you at six."

Arthur climbs the stairs to his house. He's moving awfully slowly. He'll take a nap, then maybe work on the roses. He pulls out the mail and finds a note folded over. Maddy? He opens it and reads:

I am the father of Madeline Harris. I found your address written on one of her notebooks. Please call me at 555-3376 as soon as possible.

Steven Harris

Now Arthur moves quickly into the house and to the phone.

After Lucille gets the white chocolate pudding with black-berry curd into the refrigerator, she takes off her shoes and her glasses and lies down on the sofa for a rest. The dessert looks so pretty in the wineglasses. She can hardly wait for dinner to be over so that she can serve it. Dinner is just pork roast and mashed potatoes and peas. Anyone can do that. Though she does have a way of making the outside of the roast awfully crisp and the inside awfully tender. But the pudding! People like dessert served in a wineglass. It's fes-tive. It makes a big impression. "Well, look at this!" she thinks Frank and Arthur will say. And she will wave their admiration away. It was nothing, she'll say, though that's not true. No. It's a pain in the ass to make that dessert, the way you have to stir and stir until just the right point, the way you have to strain both the pudding *and* the curd to eliminate *any* lumps. But it's worth it. The dessert is lovely to look at and absolutely delicious. She made six servings, because they'll all want seconds.

She has drifted off when the phone rings, waking her up. She thinks about ignoring it, but now that she has Frank, she isn't about to ignore a phone call.

And it is Frank on the phone, telling her he's going into the emergency room. St. Vincent's. Some chest pain, prob-ably nothing, but he might be late for dinner. Don't worry.

"I'm on the way," she says. She's begun to cry. *Stop it,* she tells herself.

"You don't have to come," he says. "I've had this happen a few times before. My nitro might be expired. They'll give me a little medication and I'll be good as new. Anyway, I'm off. I'll call you when I'm on the way over to your place."

"I'm coming," she says, but the line has gone dead.

Very calmly, she puts on her shoes and her glasses. Gets her purse. Puts down her purse to go into the bathroom to brush her teeth and put on lipstick. Comes out and grabs an AARP magazine so they'll have something to read together in the waiting room. Or the treatment room. Later, from the hospital, she'll call Arthur to let him know that dinner's off. Although maybe it won't be. Maybe they'll get Frank right in and right out. Maybe he shouldn't have that second dessert, though. She won't offer it as an option.

By the time Lucille gets into the ER, forty-five minutes have passed. She inquires at the desk and is told that he was taken right in. Thank goodness. There are so many people here! And how sick can some of them be, anyway, she wonders, sitting there playing with their phones, sleeping under their jackets, or yakking away at top volume to the people who came in with them. Laughing even louder.

"Can I go in with him?" she asks the receptionist at the desk.

"Only relatives," the receptionist says.

"I'm his fiancée," Lucille says, and the receptionist smiles what Lucille thinks is a very condescending smile. But then Lucille shows her the ring and she says, "Treatment room four. Down the hall and it will be on the right-hand side."

When Lucille is almost there, she hears *Code Blue,*

Emergency Room." They say it three times. It's not Frank. It can't be. But then she sees a red light flashing above room number four. People start flying by, someone pushing a big cart, and the door to the room is shut in her face. Absurdly— she knows it—she knocks. No one answers. She can hear some doctor inside—a woman, it sounds like—barking orders for medications.

She knocks again. "Frank?" she says, into the crack of the door. "Frank?"

Someone comes up behind her and pulls her gently by the arm, the receptionist who told her she could go in. "But I'm his fiancée," she says, and the receptionist says, "I *know,* but you can't go in there now. Let them stabilize him."

"I won't get in the way," Lucille says.

"You can't go in!" the woman says. "Please go back to the waiting room!"

So Lucille goes back to the waiting room and sits down. Her fingers are moving like they're knitting. This just can't be. No.

"Want some gum?" the woman next to her asks. Lucille takes a stick and says thank you. Shoves it in her mouth. Chews. Chews. Chews.

And now down the hall comes a middle-aged woman, panic in her face. "Frank Pearson?" she asks loudly at the desk. A low-voiced conference, and then that woman is told to take a seat, they'll call her.

The woman sits down by the vending machine, her purse balanced on her knees, staring into space. Then she starts to cry.

Lucille goes over to her. "Are you Frank Pearson's daughter? Are you Sandy?"

"Yes. Who are you?"

"I'm Lucille Howard."

Nothing.

"Frank's friend? The woman he's been seeing? His old friend? From high school?"

Again, nothing.

Lucille shows Sandy her hand. "I'm his fiancée. We just decided."

Sandy's face hardens. "You're not his fiancée!"

"I . . . But I am!"

Sandy leaps up and brushes past Lucille. At the desk, she asks what's happening with her father. Another bit of a conference, and then she goes to sit back down and Lucille knows not to approach her again. Both women sit still, waiting. After a long time, a doctor comes out of Frank's room, confers with the receptionist, and then calls out, "Mrs. Kaye?" in a very pleasant voice, as though calling her in for her massage.

"Here!" Sandy says, and strides rapidly forward.

Lucille stands. "Excuse me," she says. "I'm his fiancée?" Then, louder, "I'm his *fiancée!*" She runs down the hall after them but they're way ahead of her, and they disappear around the corner. Lucille goes back to treatment room number four and pushes open the door. The room is empty but for debris on the floor: wrappings from dressings, a syringe case, a terrible little circle of blood. Even the bed is gone. Where is he? Did they put him in the ICU? Where is he?

She sees Sandy coming down the hall and rushes up to her. "Is he all right? Where is he?"

Sandy says nothing. She walks out of the building, weeping.

Frantic, Lucille goes up to the receptionist again. "Where is Frank Pearson?"

The receptionist shakes her head sadly. Lucille drops her purse and screams.

"Thank you for this," Steven Harris tells Arthur. They are at a nearly empty Denny's close to Arthur's house, sitting at a corner booth.

"Perfectly all right," Arthur says. "How can I help?"

On the phone, Steven told Arthur that Maddy had run away. Now he says, "She calls me every day but she says she will never come home again."

"But . . . Is she here?" Arthur asks. "I mean, in town?"

"I know she's been going to school," Steven says. "She's here until school is out, couple more days, and then she says she's moving."

"Where to?"

"I don't know."

"Well, I guess I don't understand. Why don't you just go to her school and get her?"

He stares into his coffee. "I said some things to her I never should have said. And I just feel . . ."

His face takes on the kind of desperate and frozen quality

so many men's faces take on when they don't want to cry. It's a fragile fierceness, heartbreaking to behold.

He looks up, and now his face is empty of any real feeling at all; he could be a store mannequin. "I haven't been the best father. And it's too late now to try to change things. She's better off without me."

"Oh, I'm sure that's not so," Arthur says. "I'll bet if you just—"

"I was trying to find someone else who knows her," Steven says. "She never brings friends home. When I saw your address written on her notebook, I thought you might be one of the boys she . . . one of her boyfriends. But you're not, obviously." He laughs. "Unless . . . Are you?"

"No," Arthur says. "I'm just a friend. We met at the cemetery."

"The cemetery!"

The waitress comes over, a sleepy blonde who refills their cups without asking if they'd like a refill. "Anything else?" she asks, and both men say no. She slaps the check face-down on the table, as though the total is a big secret.

"Why was Maddy at the cemetery?" Steven asks. "Do you know?"

"It's near her school. She goes there on her lunch hour. Or used to. I don't see her there anymore."

Steven shakes his head. "The cemetery. She's always been an odd one. Even as a little girl. So . . . melancholy. But a cemetery!"

Arthur is a bit offended, on Maddy's behalf and his own.

"It's actually very nice there," he says. "Peaceful. I go to visit my wife there every day. Well, I visit her grave."

"Is that right?"

"Only missed one day so far and it's been seven months."

Steven sits back in the booth, crosses his arms. "My wife was cremated."

"Your wife . . . ?"

"She died when Maddy was two weeks old."

"Oh, my. My goodness. That's a hard one. Boy, oh, boy. That must have been hard."

"It never goes away. Never does."

Arthur leans forward. "The pain, you mean?"

"Yeah. But I don't like to talk about it. Or her. I never talk about her, really."

"But doesn't your daughter—"

"I don't talk about her."

Arthur nods, slowly. "I guess each person deals with death in their own way. Me, I can't stop talking about Nola. I guess it keeps her alive for me."

"Well, my wife is not alive for me anymore." Steven picks up the check, and Arthur reaches into his pocket for his wallet.

"Please," Steven says, holding up a hand. He lays a fiver on the table. "I guess I just want to ask you, if you see her . . ."

Arthur waits, wondering if he should write anything down.

"If you see her, tell her . . . Well, tell her I want to help if she needs more money. She's got some cash and a credit card, but there's a five-hundred-dollar limit. When I try to talk to her about money, she cuts me off. Or hangs up."

"You can't call her back?"

"She won't answer if she sees it's me. Has to be her calling me. She's got to run the show. She's always been that way. She's going to do what she wants to do."

She's a *child*, Arthur wants to say, but instead he says, "I'll tell her."

Arthur finds it strange that Steven didn't ask Arthur to urge Maddy to come home. He is a man who is aching and frightened and lost, that's obvious. And he may not say it, but of course he wants her to come home. If he sees Maddy, Arthur will tell her that. Although she probably knows. She sees things, Maddy. Of course her father wants her to come home! Unless . . . he doesn't?

He wonders where Maddy's staying, pictures her at some cheap motel, doing homework at the little desk. Waiting to go away. Far away. Maybe Seattle, a lot of young people go there. Or San Francisco. He hopes she'll be okay. He hopes she won't end up on the street, sitting on some worn blanket with a cardboard sign. He always wonders how that happens. Now he sees one way that happens.

At six o'clock, Arthur grabs the wildflower bouquet he's put into a Mason jar and goes over to Lucille's. He knocks, but no one answers. He peers through the glass: no lights on. No movement. No sound.

He knocks again. Well, she probably went out for a last-minute pickup of something or another. The few times he and Nola had people over for dinner, that always happened, Nola would be practically hysterical, telling him she forgot candles or she forgot whipped cream, he had to go to the store *right away*, she *had* to have them, and hurry up before the *company* came!

He decides to go home and watch for Lucille to come back. He'll toss a tinfoil ball for Gordon; he's been neglecting the cat lately. He has been neglecting him so much that Gordon has suddenly become affectionate, rubbing against Arthur's leg and so on. It doesn't suit him. It is beneath him, Arthur thinks. He can hardly wait for Gordon to normalize and become supremely indifferent again.

Arthur's not home for more than ten minutes when he sees Lucille's car come careening up her driveway. She parks crookedly, right out at the end of the driveway, doesn't pull into the garage or even close to it. The right front tire is on the lawn. Is she drunk?

He watches as the car door opens. She doesn't come out. She just sits there, her legs stuck out.

He opens his door and calls over to her. "Hey! You okay? You need any help?"

She looks at him blankly, says nothing. *Is* she drunk?

He walks slowly over to her. "Lucille?" He offers her a hand, and she takes it, stands. "Thank you, Arthur." And then, "Oh. You think there's a dinner."

"It's okay if you've changed your mind."

"Yes, I've changed my mind."

"That's fine, Lucille. But are you . . . Are you all right?"

"Well, they gave me something to calm me down. I guess I'm still a little loopy."

"Who gave you something?"

"The people at the hospital. They gave me something and they told me not to drive, but I had to come home. I had to come home."

Arthur nods. "Where's Frank?"

She begins to wring her hands. "Well, you see, that's just it. Frank *died*. He had a *heart* attack, after he told me it was *nothing* he was going in for! He said he'd see me later!"

Oh, Lord, Arthur thinks. *Oh, Lord.*

Lucille collapses in a slow-motion way onto her driveway. Arthur tries to pull her up, but she pushes him away. "No. I'm not ready to go in yet. I'm not going anywhere. I don't know where to go. I can't go in my *house,* where . . . And where the *table* is all set! I don't know where to go." She begins to cry hard. *Boo-hoo-hoo,* that's exactly what it sounds like. He guesses that's where they got it.

What to do. He asks gently, "Would you like to come to my house, Lucille?"

"No! I just want to stay right here until I decide what to do. I'm fine. You just go on home, Arthur."

Arthur goes home and gets the flowers and a blanket and some Slim Jims. He goes back outside, spreads the blanket on Lucille's driveway, puts the flowers and the Slim Jims on it. Then he lowers himself with infinite care: down on one knee, then the other, then a soft plop onto the blanket. "There," he says. "Now people will think we're just having an odd sort of picnic. You don't want the neighbors getting all alarmed and coming over."

"No, I don't."

"If someone starts to come over, why, I'll just wave to them. I'll say 'Good evening' and that we're just having a picnic. And I'll stay with you until you decide where you want to go."

"I want to go and be with Frank. That's where I want to go." She begins to weep again, though very quietly this time, and Arthur pats her shoulder.

"I'll be right here," he says. "You go right ahead and cry."

Lucille looks over at her car. "Arthur? Can you shut the door?"

"'Course I can," he says, and somehow gets up again to do it. Then he sits back down with her, a little more gingerly than before, and it hurts more this time, too. It occurs to him that it's been years since he sat on the ground. He's forgotten how things down here look, close up: the mica in the sidewalk, the ants in the grass.

He starts talking to Lucille. He tells her many things. He tells her they can sit there all night, if they want to. He tells her that she's a kind and generous woman with an optimist's heart and it's a pleasure to know her. He tells her that, when Nola first died, he thought he'd die himself, of the sorrow. He says he'd read that grief has a catabolic effect and he thought for sure it would take him right out, this immense and gnawing pain, that it would eat him alive from the inside out. But it didn't. It took a long time for him to shift things around so that he could still love and honor Nola but also love and honor life, but it happened. And it will happen to her.

"But I had love for such a short time," she says. "What a gyp! What a gyp my life has been! Really, you have to admit that, Arthur. I had someone for less than a month and now he's gone and I will never know love again!"

And then maybe Arthur makes a mistake. Because he tells her that she might meet someone else. And she begins to wail. She says, "Oh, Arthur, no one even *sees* you when you get old except for people who knew you when you were *young.*"

He guesses she's right. He stops talking. He just sits there, his eyes on her tortured face.

And then she abruptly stops crying. "Oh, well," she says. "Are you hungry, Arthur?"

"I guess I am. I'm sorry."

"Don't be sorry. I am, too. I have some pudding. Would you like some pudding?"

"Yes, thank you."

"All right." She gets herself onto her knees, and then, in a miracle of physiology, she swiftly hoists herself up to a standing position. She offers her hand to Arthur and helps him to get up. "Good thing you're so skinny," she says. "Let's go."

"Do you want to pull your car in?" he asks.

She looks over at it. "Oh. No."

"I could probably do it for you."

"I don't want to move it until morning. I don't think I can explain why."

"I understand." And he does. The car there, it's a kind of memorial service.

He grabs the flowers and follows her into the dining room, where she has set a beautiful table. Crystal. China. Silver. Cream-colored napkins, folded just so. Arthur puts his bouquet in the center of the table and sits down. *Tick . . . tock,* says the grandfather clock. *Tick . . . tock.* Arthur clears his throat against the quiet.

Lucille comes out of the kitchen with a tray on which are six glasses of white pudding topped with a beautiful burgundy-colored something.

"White chocolate pudding with blackberry curd," she says, as though she is announcing the president of the United States. She puts one glass before him, then another, then a third. He says nothing about this. He will eat every bite. Lucille puts the other three glasses at her place, sits, and lifts her spoon. And so they begin to go on.

On a hot day early in July, Arthur is at the cemetery when he hears a familiar voice. "Hey, Truluv!"

Arthur spins around so fast he nearly falls off his fold-up chair.

"Maddy!"

He's so glad to see her, he hugs her. Doesn't even think about it, just reaches over and grabs her. She stiffens, then steps back, but when he looks into her face he thinks she's pleased.

"How are you?" she asks.

"Well, I think the question, young lady, is: How are *you*?"

If how she looks is any indication, she's great. She's not so deathly pale as she was, there's a light in her eyes. And there's something else, the biggest thing: she's smiling.

"I'm good!" she says.

Should he tell her that he met with her dad? Something tells him not to. Something tells him to go slow. "Where have you been?" he asks. "I look for you every day. Once I even called you, shouted out your name really loud, probably woke up all the sleeping souls."

"Yeah, I heard you."

"You did?"

She points to the line of trees. "I was over there. I heard you, but I wasn't ready to talk to anyone. Things got bad for a while. Really bad."

"Well, I'm sorry about that, but I'm glad you're okay. I was worried about you!"

"You were?"

"'Course! We're friends, aren't we?"

She looks away, as though she's weighing the evidence.

"I'm *your* friend, anyway," he says. "And after seeing you every day and then not at all, why, I just naturally got worried."

"A lot has happened," Maddy tells him, and then falls silent.

Finally, Arthur says, "*What* has happened?" and Maddy blurts out, loudly, "Well, I'm *pregnant*, for one."

"That's . . . Are you glad?"

She looks down. "I didn't plan it, but I'm keeping it."

"A baby is a miracle. It's one of those things that everybody says, but it happens to be true."

She nods, looks at him gratefully. "Yeah, that's what I think. My dad didn't exactly feel that way. That's why I ran away."

"Where'd you go?"

Maddy laughs. "At first"—and here she makes a wide, sweeping gesture—"I came here. I slept out here for three nights. I thought I'd be scared, but I wasn't scared one bit. I was *cold*, but I wasn't scared. I washed up in the girls' bathroom every morning before school, right after the janitor got there. Then my teacher, Mr. Lyons, he asked what was up. I ran into him one morning in the parking lot on my way to the bathroom. He'd noticed I was wearing the same outfit every day, you know. . . . He's a good guy. So I just . . . Well, I told him *everything*. And told him I was going to graduate and then run away to Montana. He told me I could stay with him and Mrs. Lyons as long as I got some counseling and called my dad every day to let him know I was okay. So I've been seeing this really nice social worker and staying with the Lyonses. And being with them is like . . . I don't know. It's like I was living in a jar. With the lid on tight. And now I'm out and I never knew about all this air and all this light. You know? It's like I'd never seen in *color* before, and now I do."

"Well, that's just wonderful," Arthur says. "So are you going to marry this fellow?"

Such a bitter laugh coming from such a young woman.

"Nooooo. Nope, I'm never going to see that fellow again. Strictly a sperm donor, that's how I think of him."

"He . . . ?" Arthur doesn't know quite how to ask what he wants to without hurting her feelings.

But she answers anyway. "He wants no part of this baby. Or me. Which is fine, because I want no part of him. The social worker fixed it so he has no legal claim on the baby, not that he wanted one. But Mr. Lyons, he helped me apply to an art college that has a special dorm for single mothers! You get a roommate who's a single mother, too, and you live in a four-bedroom suite, everybody gets their own bedroom! He's pretty sure I'll get in and will even get a scholarship because of . . . Well, I write poetry and I take photographs. He sent some of my stuff to the school, and he says my chances of getting in are excellent!"

"That's great, Maddy. So you'd go this fall?"

"No, I would start the spring after the baby is born. It's due on Christmas Day."

"Oh, my. Isn't that nice! Isn't that just wonderful!"

She laughs, and he says, "*What?*" but she just shakes her head.

"So then you'll stay with your teacher until school starts?" Arthur asks.

"Well, no. I don't want to do that, even if they asked me to, which they didn't. My social worker and I have been talking about options." She looks at him. "Could I be your housekeeper in exchange for room and board? Do you need a housekeeper?"

A housekeeper! What a luxury that would be. "Why, yes, I do!" he says.

And now everything becomes delicate, somehow. And so Arthur says, "Do you do windows?" and she laughs.

"I *will*," she says.

"Why don't you bring your things over?" Arthur says. "And then we'll talk. We'll figure out your salary and whatnot, I won't have you work without a salary. I have a bedroom overlooking the front yard that you can have. You can see my rosebushes from there, did you know I have sixty different varieties? Sixty varieties and all different colors, I've even got silver! The room is painted yellow, like the sun is just pouring in there."

She says nothing.

"But you can paint it whatever color you want," Arthur says.

"I like yellow," Maddy says, and then she begins to cry. She wipes under her nose like a boy. "People are just . . . Everything has just changed so *much*," she says. And then, "Thank you, Truluv."

"Thank *you*," he says.

"Can I come over tomorrow?"

"You can come over yesterday."

She laughs. "I'll come tomorrow at around noontime. I'll take the bus."

"Tell that driver to be careful with you. Tell him you are precious cargo."

"Yeah, right. See you tomorrow!"

She walks away, and Arthur stares at the headstone. "Isn't that something?" he asks Nola. "We have a family."

And then he notices something: Mr. and Mrs. Hamburger are gone. He looks around and sees nothing. Imagine stealing something from a grave! You'd have to be pretty desperate to do something like that. Well, whoever did it, he hopes they take care of the Hamburgers. He didn't want them to ever be thrown away in his lifetime.

That night, after he eats his dinner, Arthur puts some leftovers on a plate and covers it with foil. Wieners and beans and cornbread, not so much, but something. He doctored up the beans, as usual.

He hasn't seen much of Lucille. Well, truth be told, he hasn't seen her at all. He has no idea what's going on over there, but it's time to find out.

He changes his shirt and combs his hair, inspects his teeth. As he's going out the door, he tells Gordon, "I'll be back. Guard the house. Shoot if necessary."

The cat yawns.

"You don't exactly inspire confidence," Arthur says. Now Gordon starts to head over to him and Arthur has to quick get out before the cat can escape. Too late for him to be out now.

He climbs the stairs to Lucille's house and coughs loudly, unnecessarily. He just wants to give her fair warning.

He knocks at the door. Waits.

Then he rings the doorbell, and here she comes, he can see her through the glass.

"Arthur." She's dressed in a housecoat and slippers. Her hair is all dirty, plastered to her head. Glasses crooked on her face, her flesh sagging: she's lost more weight.

"Good evening, Lucille! Have you had dinner?"

"I don't think so."

"Well, I brought you some."

She stares at the plate he's holding, and he knows she's thinking about declining his offer, so he does a dishonest thing. "Hurry up and let me put it down," he says. "It's burning my *hand*!"

Alarmed, she steps aside and he carries the dish into the kitchen. He tries not to look at the mess he passes on the way; he's never known Lucille to be a messy person, but holy mackerel. Dishes on the living room floor. Wadded-up Kleenex everywhere. Clothes tossed in the corner. A cushion from the sofa on the coffee table next to a whole slew of pill bottles. The curtains pulled sloppily shut, all wrinkled. A lamp shade askew. A terrible odor. Holy mackerel.

"Ready to eat?" Arthur asks.

"Yes," she says, but it is more like a question than an answer.

"Well, sit right down!" He takes the foil off the plate with a flourish, which is not exactly warranted by the modest offering below. Still. He pats the chair, looks at her expectantly.

She wanders over and peers down at the plate. "Oh. Hot dogs. Hot dogs and beans."

"Who doesn't like *that*?" By God, it stinks in here, too! Dishes are piled in the sink. The garbage is overflowing.

"I'm not too fond of hot dogs," Lucille says. "I never have been. Kids used to make fun of me because I didn't like hot dogs. Or ice cream. Although I do like ice cream now. And I like hot dogs *okay*." She looks over at Arthur through her filthy glasses. "I do appreciate it, Arthur. And it smells good. I guess I'm hungrier than I thought."

"Okay, so, dig in!" He motions to the chair, an elegant, sweeping motion he thinks is worthy of Fred Astaire, and she sinks into it, then looks sadly up at him. "But I have nothing for you."

"Oh, for Pete's sake," he says. "After all the things you've baked and given me?"

"Well, I guess that's right," she says. "I haven't been doing too much baking, though." She takes a bite of the beans. "Oh, my. These are awfully good. What kind are they?"

"They're Arthur Moses brand. I make 'em myself. A little catsup, a little onion, a little bacon, a little maple syrup."

"Well, they're very good," Lucille says. "You could add mustard next time, though, and that would give them a kind of barbecue flavor."

"Is that right?"

"Um-hum."

"Mustard, you say!"

"Yes, but only *French's* mustard."

See? She's perking up a little, getting bossy. He had a friend who was in AA who told him they taught the members never to get too tired, too sad, or too hungry. Bad things could happen.

He watches Lucille eat a little faster, his heart aching. It's something to feed someone who is so in need of eating. It's something to feed somebody, period.

"Would you like something to drink?" he asks.

She nods. "There's some juice in the fridge. Papaya."

He goes to look, but there's no juice. There's only milk. He picks up the container and, without opening it, can smell how bad it's gone. He puts it back and turns around to tell Lucille, "Well, no juice! But I've got a great idea. I'm going to get you a beer. Do you like beer?"

"Yes. I like a beer every now and then."

"You think a beer would taste pretty good with that hot dog?"

"Yes."

"Wait there," he says.

Arthur goes back to his house for a beer, opens it, and as he goes back out the door, Gordon slips out. "Gordon!" he calls. "Get back here. *Come!*"

Ha ha ha! says Gordon. More or less. *Ha ha,* and he runs off as fast as he can, ears back, tail straight up in the air like a ship's mast.

That coyote is still wandering around their neighborhood. "Gordon!" Arthur calls. But Gordon is at the cat bar having a cocktail. He won't be back for hours.

Arthur brings the beer into Lucille's house and is happy to see that she has finished everything.

"That was very good, Arthur," she says. "Thank you."

He hands her the beer, and she takes a long pull. "Also good," she says. She looks at the label. "Schlitz. Well, that's a nice beer."

"I like it," Arthur says. He sits down and scooches his chair closer to Lucille, puts his hand over hers.

"How are you doing, Lucille?"

She shrugs. "I'm fine."

"Have you been out at all?"

"No. I haven't been anywhere. I haven't even been out on my porch."

"Yes, I've noticed."

"I haven't even watered my garden."

"I could do that for you."

"Would you?"

"Well, of course I will. Maybe tomorrow I could water your garden, and then we could clean up a little in here?"

"Arthur, I just don't have the energy."

Frankly, Arthur doubts that he has that much energy, either. Not enough to tackle this mess.

"I know it's bad," Lucille says. "But I can't seem to do anything."

"Wait a minute," Arthur says. "I hired a housekeeper today! She's coming tomorrow. A nice girl, just graduated high school and she's on her way to art school, real nice girl. She's going to live with me and be my housekeeper until she starts college next spring. You could hire her, too!"

Lucille fiddles with the top button of her housecoat. "I don't know. I like everything just so."

Arthur looks around. Then he looks at her.

"Oh, all right," she says. "Maybe I do need help. Maybe I will hire her. How much does she charge?"

"I have no idea."

"Sounds fair to me," Lucille says, and smiles—oh, look, she is smiling!

But the stench in the kitchen is really getting to him. He feels light-headed. "Lucille, my friend," he says. "Would you like to go out on the porch?"

"I would," she says, "but I feel I should get dressed first."

"You're fine," he says. "It's dark enough."

She hesitates, pats her hair. "Maybe I'll just brush my teeth. You go ahead. Go on out there."

Arthur waits on the porch for a long time. He's just about to get up and knock on the door again when Lucille comes out. Her wig is on. Lipstick is on. A good deal of perfume is on. And she's wearing a lovely pink dress with a rhinestone belt.

Arthur stands. "Well. Lucille. You look beautiful."

"Thank you."

She sits down and begins to rock. She has shoes on with tiny little heels. Black patent heels.

"Is that a new dress?"

She nods. "Yes, I was going to wear it for my wedding." She stands up and does a slow spin. "See what it does? See what it would have done when we were dancing?"

"Very nice," Arthur says.

"Do you know what I did the day after Frank died, Arthur? I made a midnight cake and I put every pill in my house and in my purse into the batter. While it was baking, I found my old high school yearbook from senior year, and I looked at Frank and I looked at me. And then I sang some old songs. *'Gonna take a sentimental journey,'"* she sings, and her voice is surprisingly pleasant. "I tried to sing *'Smile though your heart is aching,'* but that just made me cry. I sang hymns: *'Just a closer walk with Thee.'* I sang *'All my trials, Lord, soon be over,'* and that's just how I felt, that soon all my trials would be over, and I was so happy about that, that I would know the peace that passeth all understanding.

"When the cake was done, I frosted it with a double batch of cream cheese frosting. I ate the whole thing, real fast, and the whole time I was eating, I was thinking, *God forgive me, God forgive me.* But then I threw it all up. And I sat on the bathroom floor and I . . . Well, I just emitted this *loooong* burp. The longest burp I ever heard in my life. It practically echoed off the walls."

Arthur has to restrain himself to keep from laughing out loud.

"I guess some people might think that's funny," Lucille says, and Arthur looks over to see if he's been caught out. But she's not even looking at him, she's staring off into the night. Still, he affects a deeply sorrowful expression.

"As for me, I thought it was the most mournful sound I'd ever heard. Odd and mournful, like whales singing. People say they're singing, but it sounds to me like they're keening. I think that's just how I sounded."

Now he truly is sorrowful. "Oh, Lucille. I wish you'd have called me."

She laughs. "For what? So you could watch me make a fool of myself?"

"No. So I could ask you to take a walk to look at all the flowers instead of trying to kill yourself."

She nods, then begins to rock slowly in her chair. For a long time, neither she nor Arthur speaks. Their chairs do the talking for them. Then Lucille says, "It's so embarrassing to be useless."

"Why, you're not useless!" Arthur says.

"Yes I am."

"You're just going through a hard time!"

"Yes, I am, but also I am useless. I do nothing. I realized this was happening some time ago, everything falling off, but I made do. I had church. I read books, and the paper. I had my garden. But then when Frank came into my life, well, it was like plugging in the Christmas tree. And then . . . lights off! All the lights are off now. And I really don't want to live anymore, Arthur. What is left for me now? I am useless. And so are you!"

Arthur straightens in his chair, indignant. "I'm not useless!"

"You are, too, all you do is go and visit your wife at the graveyard every single day! That's all you do!"

"Well. First of all, I don't think it's useless to visit Nola. It is my great pleasure and honor to go to the resting place of the finest woman I ever knew and think about the boundless glory of my life with her."

"Okay, I'm sorry I said that. I know how you feel about Nola. I know how much it means to you to go and visit her."

"No you don't," Arthur says. "Nobody knows how much it means to me, except maybe her. And: apart from that, I am not useless."

"But what do you *do*? You don't even go to church! You take care of your roses and that's it!"

Arthur rocks for a while. Lucille's chair has gone still, but Arthur rocks for a while.

"Let me ask you something," he says, finally.

"What."

"Did you ever hear anyone say they wanted to be a writer?"

"Yes. I've heard lots of people say that."

"*Every*body wants to be a *wri*ter," Arthur says.

"Seems like."

He stops his rocking to look over at her. "But what we need are *readers*. Right? Where would writers be without readers? Who are they going to write for? And actors, what are they without an audience? Actors, painters, dancers, comedians, even just ordinary people doing ordinary things, what are they without an audience of some sort?

"See, that's what I do. I am the audience. I am the witness. I am the great appreciator, that's what I do and that's all I want to do. I worked for a lot of years. I did a lot of things for a lot of years. Now, well, here I am in the rocking chair, and I don't mind it, Lucille. I don't feel useless. I feel lucky."

She says nothing.

"Do you know what I mean?"

"Yes, but *I* want to *do* something!" She's yelling now. And so he yells back, "Well, then, *do* it! For cripes' sake! Volunteer!"

She pushes her glasses up on her face, crosses her arms. "For your information, I looked into that. This was before Frank. This was when you were acting like you were a *saint* to sit with me for five minutes and I was dying of loneliness. Well, I decided to do something about my life. I went to the library to have them help me look for volunteer opportunities. And I'm sorry, but there was not one thing I was interested in. Hauling people to chemotherapy appointments. No. Cleaning up poop at the animal shelter. No. Teaching English, no, I just don't feel qualified for that. Serving meals to the homeless, I can't. I can't!"

"Why can't you serve meals to the homeless?" Arthur asks.

"Because I can't be on my feet that long!"

"Oh." He looks at her feet. "Do you have sneakers? They make them with Velcro straps, real easy to get on and off."

"Yes, I have sneakers! I take a ten-minute power walk every morning! Or I used to."

"Why don't you anymore?"

"I . . ." She shakes her head and sighs. "Because I am no longer interested in one single thing."

Arthur nods. Then he says, "I know this one gal, she volunteers at the hospital, answering phones at the information desk."

"Well, I can't learn all that. All that information."

"Why not?"

"Because I'm too old, Arthur! You know, it has been shown that it's harder to learn when you get older. Don't think that just because you can do a Sudoku puzzle you're in the pink! And anyway, that job would make me nervous. I'm nervous enough as it is. I've always been a nervous person, I just can't help it. Imagine, all those people crowding around the desk, asking this and that, talking over each other, coming back to complain because you gave them the wrong directions!"

"What about baking? You wouldn't have to learn anything new then, you know it all already."

She says nothing.

"Did you ever think about teaching baking, Lucille? Nobody bakes like you!"

"Well, I know that, but where am I going to teach baking? There was no listing to teach *baking* on that volunteer list."

"So what's stopping you from *putting* yourself on the list? 'Cookie baking by Lucille'?"

"I can bake far more than cookies, Arthur."

"So volunteer to teach all you know!"

Silence.

Then, "I don't know. Maybe I could. *If* I could teach right in my own house. I'm not driving *any*where."

"That's a great idea."

From the bushes over by his house, Arthur hears a loud meow. He jumps up. "I've gotta go, Lucille. Gotta get the cat in."

As he walks by her, she takes his hand and holds it. "Thank you," she says.

"That's all right. You'll be all right. You know what? Come over for lunch tomorrow, why don't you? That girl will be there. Maddy is her name. We'll have lunch, she's coming at noon. By the way, she's pregnant." He says this last part low.

"She's what?"

"Pregnant!"

"You're going to have a *baby* in your house?"

"I don't know. I guess. When she has it."

"Oh, my goodness."

"What, Lucille? You don't like babies?"

"Yes, I like babies! And I know a lot about them that I learned and never got to use! I am practically Dr. Spock!"

"Well, you'll be pretty useful then, won't you? Good night, Lucille."

He crosses over to his house and yells, "Gordon!"

The cat walks in blithe as can be. Arthur's stomach feels funny. He thinks he'd better take some bicarb and water.

After he drinks it in the kitchen, he takes a look over at Lucille's kitchen. She's sitting at the table in her pretty dress, with her wig off.

Lucille sits at the kitchen table, tapping a pencil against a blank recipe card on which she was going to make a list of pros and cons. But she wonders if she should just go ahead and do what Arthur suggested. There are so many recipes she could share. Though not the orange blossom cookie one. Or the lavender shortbread. No. Never. And she'd hate to give out the lemon drop cheesecake recipe, then everyone will have it. Then again, why not? She can teach so many people so many things! They will ask questions. They will ask for her approval. She will be a teacher again, but to adults this time, like a professor. She will be a source of inspiration to so many people whose idea of good cake is Duncan Hines, for heaven's sake. She will teach them to make things they've never heard of that they'll love. They'll love them!

She looks at the dying philodendron in the corner of the kitchen. She gets a glass of water and carefully pours some in the dirt. A plant in the kitchen is cheerful. It would be a shame to let it go. She will not let it go.

She settles herself back in her chair. Well. Here is the situation. She is ingloriously, indubitably here. Might as well be useful.

Frank, saying, *Who cares what happens before we're born and after we die? The question is, what do we do in the meantime?*

Pistachio party cake, she writes on the card. That will be the first one she teaches, because it's so easy. She'll start them off with ingredients they're familiar with. Already, she knows what she'll wear that day: her pistachio-colored blouse. Nearly the same color as the cake. And her first question: "Who here has never sifted flour?" A few hands, a few shameful looks. "Now, don't feel bad, this is why I'm here. I'm going to pass around this sifter, it's an oldie but goodie. Try it out. You'll get the hang of it right away."

Pinwheels. Maple cake with maple syrup frosting. Cocoa marshmallow cake. Lemon snaps. Jelly roll. Pudding cake. Apricot bars. Marigold cake, oh, that's a light one, you just feel like it will float right off the fork.

In fact, she'll make one tomorrow and bring it over for their lunch! She gets up to go to bed, and sees all the dishes in the sink. Lord! Well, she's still here. She'll get to them in the morning.

Maddy drops her duffel bag in the middle of the bedroom. Arthur showed her up there, then asked if she'd like to be alone to settle in. "Maybe for just a few minutes," she told him. Yes. She wants to feel this place out.

She likes the dark color of her solid wooden bedroom door, and she loves the glass doorknob. The walls are indeed painted a pale yellow color that looks like a wash of sun. There are white see-through curtains, but window shades, too, a bit yellowed with age, but when she tests them they work perfectly fine. There's a single bed against the wall, a white flowered chenille bedspread over it. Only one pillow, but she'll get more. She sits at the edge of the bed, bounces up and down to test the firmness. It's a bit soft, which she actually likes a lot.

There's a round rag rug on the floor, done in colors of

pink and yellow and blue. In the corner is a little uphol-
stered chair, pink velvet. Worn, but very appealing. Next to
it is a lamp from around 1812, from the looks of it. Maddy
tries the switch. It works. She sits in the chair and discovers
that it rocks. Perfect.

A wooden desk is against another wall, a kind of clunky
old thing, but with deep drawers. Maddy goes to sit in the
desk chair and opens a drawer. There's a receipt in there:
Arthur bought it yesterday from the Goodwill. Sixty dollars
for both the desk and chair. She'll pay him back out of her
first paycheck.

Next to the desk is a little white bookcase, empty now;
she guesses Arthur removed everything so she could fill it
with whatever she wants. She has only a few books: a couple
of slim volumes of poetry, Jane Hirshfield and Barbara
Crooker, which Mr. Lyons gave her; and a great big book of
Walker Evans's photography, *American Photographs*, which
she took with her when she left home. It was a gift from her
father one Christmas; Maddy had begged and begged for it
after she had seen it in the library. It was the only thing she
wanted.

She looks at the inscription inside the Evans book: *For
Maddy, Merry Christmas from your father.* It is only now that
she realizes how odd it is that he didn't say *Love.* It's something she and her counselor talk about, how broken her dad
is. And how the onus is on *him* to get fixed.

She'll get more books. They're really cheap at yard sales,
they practically pay you to take them. She'll get more books,
she'll take care of her baby, and she'll be the best student

that art college has ever seen, they will never regret having given her a scholarship. She never knew such a school existed. One hundred and eleven miles away. She has always said that eleven is her lucky number.

Also, she will be the best housekeeper Arthur has ever seen. She actually looked up housekeeping tips online, including how to iron.

Online!

Maddy calls down to the kitchen, where Arthur is preparing lunch. Chili dogs, they're having. He's down there chopping up onions, she can smell them.

"Arthur!" she calls.

He appears at the bottom of the steps, a dishtowel tucked into his pants, a little paring knife in his hand. "Yes?"

"Are you online?"

He cups his hand around his ear. "Say again?"

"Are you *online*?"

"Yes, I have a clothesline. Right out back. Washer and dryer are in the basement, by the way."

"No, are you *online*?"

He frowns. "Am I fine? Is that what you're asking?"

She comes halfway down the stairs and says, "Arthur, do you have a computer?"

"Oh. No."

"Okay. I can use one at the library."

"Well, I could get a computer."

He'd never use it, and she'll be gone soon. "If I decide I need one here, I'll pay for it out of my salary," she tells him.

Her salary. Maddy relishes the negotiation they had:

MADDY: Room and board is all I need.

ARTHUR: Absolutely not. I'm going to pay you. How's fifty dollars a day?

MADDY: Fifty dollars a day! That's fifteen hundred dollars a month!

ARTHUR: Oh. Is it?

MADDY: Yes!

ARTHUR: (worried-looking) Sixty dollars a day?

MADDY: Truluv. If you pay me sixty dollars a month it will be fine. It will be more than enough. There's that scholarship, remember?

ARTHUR: Four hundred dollars a month, and that's my last offer.

"The chili smells good," Maddy says.

"Hormel."

"There you go."

"Are you almost ready to eat?" he asks.

"Sure. And remember: from now on, I cook."

Arthur smiles.

The doorbell rings and he says, "Oh, I forgot to tell you, I invited my neighbor Lucille over for lunch. She's bringing dessert. She's quite the baker."

"Yes, you gave me some of her orange blossom cookies."

"Oh. That's right. I remember."

Maddy thinks he does not, but so what.

She goes back to her room and hangs up her few clothes in the closet. Way in the back is something . . . Oh. A crib. A really old, folded-up crib, with a lamb resting on pink and blue clouds painted on the headboard. So this would have been the baby's room. She touches the crib gently, then rests her empty duffel in front of it.

Maddy takes the beat-up photo of her mother from her purse and props it up on the wall behind her desk, then goes downstairs.

Before they are even introduced, Lucille says, "Well, look at you! Talk about the glow of pregnancy!"

So Lucille knows. It's a relief, in a way. "I'm Maddy Harris," she says, and offers her hand. Lucille shakes it with a vigor Maddy would not have predicted.

"I'm so pleased to meet you," Lucille says breathlessly. "I'm Lucille Howard, your next-door neighbor." She points to her house. "That one. Right there."

"Yes, Arthur has told me about you."

Lucille looks quickly over at Arthur.

"He told me you're a really good baker. I had some of your orange blossom cookies, and they were amazing."

"Oh. Well. Thank you. But wait till you taste *that*!" She points to a cake in the center of the table, frosted a vibrant orange color, frosting flowers ringing the edges. Marigolds, Maddy thinks they're supposed to be.

"Let's eat before anything gets cold," Lucille says. And then, spying the water that Arthur has set out for all of them, she turns to him and says, "Don't you have *milk*? She needs *milk*. She's carrying a *child*. She needs *calcium*! The little *bones*!"

Arthur looks a bit flustered. "Well, let me look."

He starts to get up, and Maddy puts her hand over Arthur's. "It's okay. I'll drink water for now. I like water with chili dogs."

"Well, exactly," Arthur says. "And beer."

"She can't have *beer!*" Lucille practically screeches, and Maddy says, "I know that, Lucille."

Old bat. And yet how wonderful to be paid attention to. How wonderful to be cared for, even if it's by a couple of goofy old people. She adores Arthur. Arthur and his things, like Mr. and Mrs. Hamburger. Who are in her backpack. Later tonight, she'll confess. Here's what she knows: he'll forgive her.

Lucille lowers the shade in her bedroom and flops down on the bed. Oh, the sheets smell sweet. Maddy washed the sheets and ironed the pillowcases, now where are you ever going to find someone to do that.

She also took out all the trash and dusted and vacuumed and swept like Cinderella. She did all the dirty dishes and wiped them and put them away. She watered the garden and the houseplants. She stacked up all the mail into a neat little pile. She threw things out of the refrigerator and wiped down the shelves. She was supposed to clean Arthur's place, but Arthur said 'Ladies first,' and so there you are, Lucille is going to bed knowing that in the morning she will come down into the kitchen, where everything is back to normal, only better. Shining! Maddy put a bouquet of tulips on her dining room table, and she even put one in the bathroom in a little aspirin bottle. Lucille would rather not see that aspirin bottle. But the tulip almost makes her forget why the bottle is empty.

She's such a delicate thing, Maddy. She's tall, but slight. She's like a little bird, and she arouses Lucille's protective instincts. Such a wonderful girl, if she'd just take that thing out of her nose. Lucille didn't see any tattoos, but she understands that a lot of kids put them in nasty places: she supposes the girl could have one, all right.

But she is awfully pretty. Smart, courteous, quick to laugh, and observant, truly observant. And the kind who can anticipate things you might need. She doesn't talk much to Lucille, most of her remarks are directed at Arthur. But she can clean.

And she *loved* Lucille's cake. She practically fainted after she tasted it. "Ohhhhhhhh," she said after the first bite, her eyes closed, and it was one of those sounds like she was in pain, but she wasn't in pain, she was in ecstasy. Well, the cake *is* special. Even for Lucille. "How did you *make* this?" Maddy asked, and Lucille did her usual and waved her hand and said it was nothing. Well, it was not nothing! *Twice*-sifted flour, whole nutmeg grated on that irritating little grater that almost always scrapes her knuckles. You think it's easy making frosting marigolds? One compromise is that the frosting was tinted by food coloring (organic) and not calendulin, which of course is what gives marigolds their astonishing color. But she didn't have any marigolds. And anyway, you have to watch what you eat when you're carrying a baby. A pregnant woman she knows from church told

Lucille the only thing hard about being pregnant was that she couldn't eat sushi. *Hard?* Lucille thought. She herself would be dancing in the streets if she were told she must not eat sushi.

Lucille closes her eyes. Let's see, what else did they say about the cake? Oh, how light it was; of course, they commented on the lightness, anyone who has ever had that cake has commented on the lightness. All those egg whites, whipped with a whisk by hand before adding to the batter, because then you can be absolutely precise about the texture and the amount. The recipe may say add six egg whites, but what Lucille always thinks about any instruction in any recipe is: *We'll see about that.* She also hand-whipped the cloudlike whipped cream she served with the cake. Marigold cake doesn't want ice cream, it's too delicate. It wants a nice-size plop of whipped cream, just off to the side. Most people put too much vanilla in whipped cream. Other people don't use it at all. They're both wrong. Use just a kiss. Lucille makes small cuts on a vanilla bean and uses it to stir the cream. If that's not quite enough, she dips a toothpick into double-strength vanilla and stirs that in. Voilà.

Only once did Lucille think of Frank and all he was missing during this lunch. Only once did she think exactly that: *Oh, Frank, look what you're missing.* Although if Frank were still alive, it's entirely possible she wouldn't have been at this lunch. It's probable she wouldn't have been.

Isn't life funny. It could drive you crazy if you thought about it too much. Turn this way and that happens. Turn that way and this happens.

A baby on the way! She'll have to keep a sharp eye out. She'll have to be over there all the time to make sure things are being done right for that little one, whom she thinks she will secretly call Emma Jean. That's what she named her favorite doll when she was a child, after her best friend, Emma Jean Beanblossom, and that's what she had wanted to name a daughter. Yes, she'll call the baby Emma Jean in her mind, no one needs to know. It *is* a girl. Lucille is certain of this. She has predicted the sex of at least ten babies and not once has she been wrong.

She'll offer to cook for them. No more lonely meals for her and Arthur, and she can make sure Emma Jean is properly nourished. There must be cookbooks for babies. If not, she'll write one. Now that she's back in teacher mode.

Her first class is in three days. She put an ad up in the grocery store, in the library, and at the Walmart on the outskirts of town:

BACK TO BAKING WITH LUCILLE

Why buy store bought when you can make your own? Baking from scratch costs less, means more to people, tastes better, and it's not as hard as you think. Participants will start with the basics and progress to fancy desserts that will impress all. Learn with a pro. You won't be sorry.

So far she has two fish on the line. Certainly not as many as she was hoping for, but she will be gracious to those who did sign up. It's not their fault more people don't have the good sense to take advantage of an offer like this. Word will spread. She might even get interviewed for the local paper. In fact, she might as well buy the outfit she'll wear for that now, before it gets too busy. They should photograph her at the kitchen table, with a nest of mixing bowls nearby. A block of butter, a pile of chocolate squares, unwrapped, but with the paper still on them for an artistic touch. And a finished chocolate cake on her beautiful floral cake platter. They should take a few different angles, and refrain from any close-ups of Lucille. They should put the picture on the front page, because it would help sell copies. People love to look at food, especially chocolate cake.

At seven o'clock in the evening on the day of her first class, Lucille is lying in bed, exhausted. One thing she now knows for sure is that you can't tell people anything. No. People have lost their ability to concentrate, to pay attention. They also have lost their manners. Hello? Have you ever heard of *please* and *thank you*? Although on the way out, holding a boxed-up, very generous slice of the delicious pistachio party cake Lucille had helped her make, her student (only one of the two signed up had come) had said, "Okay, well, thanks."

She was a fortyish woman, a kind of blowsy-looking blonde named Trudy. She kept eyeballing her phone on the table beside her, even though Lucille asked her very nicely to turn it off. She said she couldn't turn it off but she wouldn't answer it. And then didn't it just whistle or buzz or play some stupid tinny song every five minutes. Who did people think they were, anymore, that they could never turn off their phones?

Lucille had to repeat instructions over and over, the woman could hardly crack an egg. She didn't want to whip anything by hand; she had the gall to say, "There's a new thing called a mixer." And then Lucille had to keep calm and carry on and say, "Ha, that's funny, but you know what? You have so much more control with a whisk." Then, attempting a little humor, she said, "And it's good exercise!" And Trudy said, all smug-faced, "Well, I go to a private Pilates class, so . . ."

"Isn't *that* great?" Lucille said, seething. And then she made Trudy use the whisk; she shoved it in her hand and put her own hand over it and said grimly, "Okay, here we go." And Lucille had the kindness not to gloat when Trudy saw how well it worked. "Wow," she said, and Lucille said, "See what you did?" just like she used to with her kids in school.

There were some nice moments. While the cake baked, Lucille taught Trudy certain substitutions that always worked, what to do when adding spices so you didn't forget if you'd added this or that, why you should freeze butter wrappers to grease pans. She was glad to see that Trudy took notes in the little pad Lucille had given her. Best of all, Lucille supposes, she is coming back next week and she is bringing along two friends for the chocolate soufflé class. *If* they have time, Trudy cautioned; they're very busy.

Lord. This is going to be harder than she thought.

She looks over at Arthur's house and sees so many lights on. It makes her a little jealous. She wonders if there will be a bedroom set aside for the baby, even though she won't be there long. Arthur has all that room, four bedrooms, just like she does. After Nola died, Lucille wondered why he didn't sell that house. Well, what about her? Why didn't she sell her house? Her parents left her a nice inheritance, and she bought her house because she thought it was charming and that eventually she'd need all that space, but she never did. Lots of closed doors. And if there's anything that makes you feel lonely, it's a lot of closed doors in your own house.

She should sell her house. She should sell it and move in with Arthur and teach her classes over there. They could have a kind of commune. She could cook, Maddy could clean, and Arthur could tend to the garden and take out the garbage. And squash any spiders that came in, although knowing Arthur, he wouldn't squash them, he'd put them back outside. Well, fine. Arthur can be in charge of insect removal, method totally up to him. And mice. Though he has a cat, so that probably isn't much of a problem. A mouse ran across Lucille's kitchen floor last winter, and she climbed right up on a chair, just like a cartoon person, she climbed up there and screamed, *"Get out! Get out! Get out!"* and then cried and then smacked the thing with her broom until she killed it. Which she still feels bad about.

But really, they might as well live together. It's been done before, those hippies and their communes. And it was done before that, too, families used to always live together, babies and parents and grandparents all under one roof. Unmar-

ried aunts and uncles. There weren't so many sad old people like . . . Well, like her and Arthur, standing at their
windows and looking out. Making coffee for one every
morning. There were none of those god-awful holding pens
that they try to pass off as some sort of social club (not to say
sex club, don't think Lucille hasn't heard stories) for the el-
derly that charged an exorbitant amount of money and then
raised the rent every ten minutes. They're everywhere now!

Her friend Charlotte moved into one of those places
when she turned eighty-two, and she told Lucille it was the
biggest mistake she ever made. "Do you know what happened the first day I moved in?" she asked Lucille. "My
next-door neighbor presented me with a housewarming gift
of an undone wire hanger because the toilet always gets
blocked up. She said I might as well have it right away, they
all used them, and they were the only things that worked."
And then Charlotte died within a year. She wasn't sick when
she went in there, either.

Lucille will never live in one of those stupidly named
places, their names were all stupid. Brookdale when there
wasn't a brook for miles. Crestwood. Crestwood! What did
that mean? And inside, all the same kind of person, everywhere you looked. No. She'd rather rot in her house. Or in
Arthur's house. They can rot together, there's something
nice about rotting together. Though of course you wouldn't
say it that way. You'd say there's something nice about heading into what are inarguably the final few years of your life
in the company of one kind person, who can relate to all
that you're going through, and vice versa.

She'll suggest it. She'll go slowly, make a little, subtle suggestion, and let him think he thought of it. That was men. You had to make them think they thought of things and then they were more likely to do them.

She closes her eyes, and thinks of Frank. Here and gone, just like that. Oh, you couldn't count on anything, really. You had to seize the moment, act on a good impulse before everything just disappeared. Before you yourself disappeared. She picks up the phone and calls Arthur.

When he answers groggily, she says, "Can I move in with you? With you two? I'll be the cook and I'll pick up all the groceries and pay for them, too. And I'll pay rent."

"You . . . ? Well, I don't know. But you wouldn't have to pay rent, don't be silly."

"I'd help with everything. Listen, Arthur, a girl needs another woman around when she's pregnant, believe me. So, what do you say?"

"Well . . . I *guess* so."

"Oh, thank you, Arthur! What a good idea. Won't we have fun?"

She hears him yawn.

"I could move in tomorrow! I'll bring a few small things and then I'll call EZ Move, I've seen those young men around the neighborhood, they have the nicest uniforms. I don't think they speak English, but they certainly will understand that I want to move, or I can pantomime."

Silence, and the sound of deep breathing.

"Arthur?"

"Hello?"

"Are you sleeping?"

"No!"

"So, I'll move in tomorrow."

"All right, Lucille."

"Until then!"

She hangs up the phone and sits still, her eyes wide. *Until then!* As though she's Myrna Loy, tossing a mink stole seductively over her shoulder on the way out the door. So foolish! But Arthur didn't seem to think so. He's calm water, that one.

She won't sell her house right away, of course. She'll just have those men move over her baking supplies and her clothes and her bed. Some pictures for the walls. A few other things. Not much. Maybe her piano and her grand-father clock.

She lies back down and closes her eyes. She will teach her classes and shop for groceries and cook. Maddy will clean and do the laundry. And Arthur will tend the roses and prevent animal abuse.

Early the next morning, Lucille calls a realtor. Just for an appraisal, she tells the agent, Rhonda House, and isn't that funny, but it's true, her last name is House! But Rhonda House knows a few things about people who call for just an appraisal and she's practically licking her chops. She knows Lucille's house very well. That's a nice place! Assuming the inside isn't a wreck, Rhonda can sell it in five minutes.

———

At nine o'clock, when Arthur comes downstairs for breakfast, Maddy is cleaning the kitchen. She has on jeans and a T-shirt and a bandanna wrapped around her head, and Arthur thinks she looks beautiful. "Morning!" she says, and Arthur smiles and nods. He's not much of a talker in the morning until he's had his coffee. Actually, he's not that great a talker, period. He's a quiet man. He was a quiet boy and he's a quiet man.

He goes over to pour himself coffee from the pot Maddy has made—how nice not to have to make your own coffee!—and sits down at the table. "This is good," he says.

"Thanks," Maddy says, and then she keeps quiet, just continues scrubbing the stove as though he isn't there. Well, isn't that nice! Rare thing for a woman, Arthur thinks.

Nola used to get perturbed with his quiet. "*Oh!*" she'd say, sometimes. "I just wish you'd make yourself a little *livelier!*" Once when she said that, it was at dinner and he rose up from the table, took in a deep breath, and yodeled good and loud for a full half minute. And Nola stared at him in amazement. "I didn't know you knew how to yodel!" she said. And he said, "Now you do." "*Why* didn't I know you could yodel?" she asked, and he said it didn't really come up that much, the need to yodel.

Arthur watches Maddy work, and he realizes that an essential loneliness he had is abating. He didn't notice it as much when it was there as he does now, when it is lessening. Isn't that funny. He doesn't want to get too attached to her; she'll be leaving, and then he'll be alone again. It makes for a sinking feeling, until he remembers that Lucille is moving in. And that makes for another kind of feeling. Panic.

"Maddy?"

She turns around.

"I have to tell you something."

She comes to the table, sits across from him. He sees that she is worried, like she's done something wrong, and it breaks his heart.

"I'm so glad you're here," he says.

Now she brightens.

"But I want to tell you that Lucille called last night, and she . . . Well, she would like to move in with us. I told her she could. I hope that's okay with you."

Maddy says nothing.

"Is it okay?"

She shrugs. "I mean, it's your house, right?"

Arthur crosses his skinny legs, leans back in his chair. "All right then."

Well, he's a dead duck now. He's gone and made everything official and he isn't even sure if he's sure. What if it doesn't work out? Then he'll have to tell Lucille to leave and maybe drive her over the edge.

Or! He could get used to her and then she could want to leave and then what? Or she could die. Or he could die.

Enough!

Maddy has said something and is looking at him expectantly.

"What was that?"

"Would you like more coffee before I go upstairs?"

"I'd love some."

Maddy gets up to grab the pot of coffee and refills his cup. And he is content.

Long after Arthur has showered, Maddy is still in her room. Arthur climbs the stairs and knocks at the door. No answer, but she's in there, he knows. He can hear her in the quiet; he can very nearly see her: head bowed, hands clasped, breathing shallowly. He knocks again, then speaks into the crack of the door. "Maddy? If you want to be by yourself, I'm going to let you be by yourself. But if you wouldn't mind talking to me, I'd sure like to talk to you."

Nothing. He waits with the unperturbed patience that is given to many older people. He stares at the door, thinking it could use a varnishing. He examines his hands: front, back. He listens to the cardinal whistling outside and to the distant sound of a lawnmower, and gives thanks for his hearing aids. He wonders what's for lunch.

Finally, he says into the crack, "Okay then, I'll just be downstairs somewhere. You let me know if you need anything."

Now she opens the door. She is wearing her jacket and holding her duffel bag. Her bed has been stripped; the linens are folded neatly at the bottom of the bed. She sees him looking over at the bed and says, "I didn't sleep in those sheets. I'd just put them on this morning."

"What are you doing, Maddy?"

"Moving out."

"Why?"

"Lucille is moving in, right?"

"Well, yes, but that doesn't mean —"

"I figured if she was moving in, I should move out."

"But why?"

Nothing.

Then she says, "I need to get to the bus stop."

"Where are you going?"

She doesn't answer, just stares at the floor.

Arthur gestures toward the inside of her room. "Can we sit and talk for a minute?"

She hesitates, then moves to sit on the side of her bed. Arthur sits at the desk.

He clears his throat. "I would never ask you to do anything you didn't want to do. But I guess I don't understand why you want to leave. I thought you were happy here."

She nods. "I was."

"So . . ."

"I just don't see why she needs to move in. She lives next door! Why does she have to live here with us?"

Arthur nods. "I kind of wondered that myself. After I hung up from talking to her, I lay wide awake in my bed, thinking, *Oh, boy, now look what I've done.*"

Maddy relaxes a bit from the stiff posture she had assumed, her back ramrod straight, her chin up defensively.

"I thought, that woman minds everybody's business," he goes on. "She'll be telling me how much cream to put in my coffee and how tight to buckle my belt. When to go to bed and when to get up. If I want to have a little thinking time in my room, she'll come barreling in like the *Queen Mary* asking what am I thinking about, then telling me whether or not I *should* be thinking about it."

Maddy crosses her arms. "So . . . ?"

Arthur holds up his hand. "Wait a minute. Let me finish some of the horrors I've envisioned. She'll be taking over the kitchen entirely."

Maddy shrugs. "Well, she is a good cook."

"She'll be blabbing on and on about her exploits at the beauty parlor and the grocery store, sharing all the gossip she gets. Bringing *people* over here for classes, invading our privacy! And you know, she wants to have little kids in here! Beginning Baking, she said, she's going to teach them how to make lollipops! You ever hear a group of children laughing? They'll blow the roof off this place!"

Maddy says nothing.

But then Arthur says, "But you know what? Here's the thing. You know what else I thought about after I said yes— I admit, without even really thinking about it?"

"What." She is looking out the window, but she's listening.

"I thought about how she might have lived a long time being afraid in the night—she always leaves so many lights on. She believes that her last chance for love just died, and her last chance was her first love, and there is something about that that is awfully hard to bear. Think about it. To know you're at the end of hoping for love and to realize that something else will have to do, if you're going to have any reason to go on.

"I guess what I decided is that Lucille is like a pink tank.

You know? She's a tank, but she's pink. And I think if she gets on our nerves too much we can just tell her. She can take it. What's the worst that can happen? She'll throw a cupcake at us?"

Silence, until Gordon comes into the room and meows.

"Okay if he's here?" Arthur asks.

Maddy doesn't answer, but she pats the bed beside her and the cat jumps up.

"His vote is that you please stay here. His vote is that you don't go any more than five feet from him. Ever."

"I know," Maddy says, stroking the giant head.

"Sounds like an outboard motor when he purrs, doesn't he?"

She smiles.

Arthur stands. "Well, I'm going over to give Lucille the bad news."

Maddy looks up. "What do you mean?"

"I can see you're not comfortable with her living with us. That's all right, I'm glad you told me. And so I'm going over to tell her she can't move in after all. I'll tell her I made a mistake. And I did make a mistake. I should have talked about it with you first. I apologize. I'll go tell her and then maybe we can have some lunch, just the two of us."

He gets up to go to the door.

"Truluv," she says.

He turns around.

"You think I don't know what you're doing?" Gordon is in her lap now, upside down, his eyes closed.

"I will tell her not to move in, Maddy. If her moving in means your moving out."

Maddy waves her hand. "Oh, let her come." Her knee is jiggling a mile a minute.

Arthur waits until she looks up at him.

"You sure?"

"Yeah." She laughs. "Yeah, let her come. I'll stay."

"Want me to help you unpack?"

"No, I got it. I didn't get too far. It's mostly just a couple of books and some shirts in there."

"Can I tell you something, Maddy?"

"Sure."

"We used to have some real good friends, Nola and I, named Tom and Joanie Guthrie. Married the same month and year as we were, and we always thought we'd have kids at the same time and they could play together; Tom and I talked all the time about building swing sets and sandboxes.

"Well, Nola and I couldn't have kids, as you know, so we kind of made our friends' children our own. They had the one, little Bobby, and then four years later Joanie had another son, named him Clyde. Bobby couldn't seem to say Clyde and called him Kite, and we all loved that; fact, it became his nickname. But anyway, what I want to tell you is that when Joanie had that second baby, she seemed awfully blue. And she finally told Nola that she was so worried about whether she could love two children, about whether she could make room in her heart for as much love as she felt for Bobby. Wasn't it betraying Bobby, to love another child? And Nola told her what her sister Patricia had said, after having *her* second. Patricia said she felt like she'd grown a second heart."

"Okay, Truluv," Maddy says.

"Okay?"

"Yes. Thank you."

He starts to leave the room and she says, "Truluv? Hold on a second, I have something to tell you."

"Oh?"

She goes into her closet and emerges holding Mr. and Mrs. Hamburger.

"*There* they are!" Arthur says, and the joy makes his voice crack. "Where'd you find them?"

"I took them," Maddy says, her head down. "I took them off Nola's grave." She looks up, serious-faced and a little pale, too, he thinks. He'll talk to Lucille about that, later. More spinach in her diet? Liver?

"I'm very sorry," Maddy continues. "I'll put them back today. I just . . . I really like them, and I thought I might not see you again and so I just took them. I'm really sorry."

"You like them, huh?" Arthur says.

She nods. "They're so retro!"

"Well, you want to know something funny? I was going to give them to you for your birthday. So, Happy Birthday."

"*Really?*"

You'd think he was giving her the Eiffel Tower.

"Really."

She goes over to her desk and places the Hamburgers on the corner. She steps back to regard them, then makes a minor adjustment. "There!"

Next she goes to her duffel bag and takes out a small photograph that she puts next to the Hamburgers. Arthur goes over to inspect it. "You?" he asks.

"No, that's my mom."

"Oh!" Arthur says, and takes another, long look. "Died when you were only two weeks old. That's a shame."

Maddy's voice changes, goes deeper. "How do you know that?"

Uh-oh. He turns around to face her. "Well, I met your dad, actually. I meant to tell you. He got my address from that time you wrote it down, and after you ran away, he left me a note asking me to call him. I did, and we met. He was afraid for you. And he wanted to get a message to you."

"What message was that?"

Tell her I want to help if she needs more money. "He wanted you to come home. He loves you and he really wanted you to come back."

She looks levelly at him. "He said that?"

"Well, of course he did. More or less, I mean, I don't re-call the exact words. But of course he did. I think he's very sorry about how . . . I think he's sorry."

"Yeah, well, I'm not going back there. All done with that. I can't go back. It's not healthy for me, okay?"

"Okay. But he knows you're here, right?"

"He knows I'm here."

Arthur peers more closely at the photograph. "Beautiful woman."

"Yes."

"It must have been hard for your dad, that you look so much like her."

"Or he could have been glad that he still had some part of her, through me," Maddy says. "That's what my counselor says, and that's what I think, too."

She's quiet for a moment, and then she says, "Can I tell you something?"

"Of course!"

"I want to tell you, because I think you'll understand."

"Okay. I'm all ears. Plus, I'm all ears." He points to his oversize ears. He sits back down at the desk, and Maddy goes back to the bed.

"So, this is kind of a weird story. When I was about four years old, I told my dad I wanted to die."

Arthur inhales sharply, and Maddy says quickly, "It wasn't . . . It wasn't because I was sad or anything like that. It was that I'd been taught about heaven and hell in Sunday school, and I thought heaven seemed like such a wonderful place. And my dad had told me my mother was there. I'd been told about sin, too, about how sins stained your soul. I thought of it like flypaper, all this black stuck onto white. It seemed to me that as I got older, my sins would get bigger, so the best thing might be to die young, and then I'd be pretty much guaranteed admission into heaven.

"So I told my dad about it one day, he was reading the paper at the kitchen table and I came up and stood very close to him, he didn't like for you to talk to him when he was reading the paper. But eventually he pulled me onto his lap, which he hardly ever did, but he did that day, and he said, 'What's up?' And I said, 'I want to die,' said it very happily, I think, I mean, I was just so happy about the idea. And he . . . he just went *nuts*! He pushed me off his lap and started yelling. He said, 'Nobody asks to be born! *Nobody!* You get here and you just have to deal with what you get!'

"I didn't know what to do. I didn't understand why he was so angry. I thought he'd be glad. I'd be with my mother and I'd be out of his hair. I always felt like a burden to him. I always felt he'd be glad not to have me around, reminding him every day of the wife he no longer had. I think he loved my mother an awful lot. I think that was a good love. But he lost her. Because of me. And when he lost her, something spoiled in him. And then he lost himself."

Arthur starts to speak, and Maddy holds up her hand. "I know. I know it wasn't my fault. But boy, it sure felt that way. Every day, it sure felt that way."

Arthur nods. His hands are clasped in his lap, and he runs one thumb over the other. He says, "I don't know what to say about that, Maddy, except to say that I think your father said the wrong thing. I think he should have held you tight and told you what a marvelous little philosopher you were, and that heaven would be waiting for you a long, long time from then. It must have been awfully hurtful and confusing to such a little girl to hear him say those things to you, to push you off his lap the way that he did. But the longer I live, the more I come to see that love is not so easy for everyone. It can get awfully complicated. It can make us do good things but it can also make us do bad things. One thing I know, though, is that your dad must have done some things right. Because look at you. Look how you turned out. And I would bet my last nickel that your dad loves you very much, Maddy."

Her eyes fill, and he wants to say more, but the doorbell rings and they hear Lucille sing out, "*Yoo-hoo!*"

Arthur and Maddy look at each other.

Then, "I got it," Maddy says grimly, and heads downstairs. Arthur moves to the open closet door and peers in. One pair of shoes, or rather a kind of boot. A pair of jeans and a pair of sweatpants. Three tops. A jacket, one of those Army fatigue jackets that the kids seem to like so much. That's it. And— What the? "Get out of there, Gordon!" The cat flicks his tail and stays crouched firmly in place. "Suit yourself," Arthur says.

"I'll take that," he hears Maddy say.

"Okay," Lucille says. "Now, be careful, that's all my extracts, they cost a fortune." Then, "No, no, I can handle my suitcase. It's light. The movers will be here tomorrow. Do you know what room is mine?"

"I'll show you," Arthur says from the staircase. And his old heart jumps in his chest.

He'll put her in Nola's sewing room. Small, but light-filled. Flowered wallpaper that Arthur himself put up years ago. He cut his finger that day. Nola made hamburger soup and yeast rolls for dinner. So funny the odd details you remember.

On the shelf of the closet is Nola's sewing machine. He'd

like to keep it there. Lucille won't mind, he doesn't think. She can use it, if she wants. Though if he hears that machine running it might kill him dead because it will bring back the memory of him and Nola buying that machine to make baby clothes, then Nola using it for everything but. Still, Lucille can use it if she wants.

Arthur ushers her into the room, and she looks around. "Wallpaper's peeling," she says. "Would you mind if I fix that?"

"Okay with me," Arthur says. "I don't think they make that pattern anymore, though."

"Well . . . maybe I could paint it?"

"I guess that would be all right."

"Oh, good! I know exactly the color I want. I saw it in Dooley's Hardware not long ago, and I thought to myself, *Oh, do I wish I had a need for that!* It's called Bakery Box Pink, isn't that just perfect? You'll feel like you're in a bakery every time you come to my room!"

There goes the neighborhood, Arthur thinks. Going in her room will probably feel like being trapped in a bottle of Pepto-Bismol, but never mind, it's her room now. Let all these personalities reveal themselves. When Nola was alive, he lived by her decorating rules, anything she wanted was fine with him. But now he's on his own. And you know what? From the time he was a little boy, he has wanted a saddle in his room. A Western saddle on a fence. He could have a little fence built in the corner of his room and go and buy a saddle to toss over it. If the baby's a boy, why, he'll love it. He can sit up there and pretend to be riding the range.

For that matter, if the fence is built low and sturdy enough, and the saddle is glued firmly into place, Arthur could try it himself. Don't think he wouldn't.

At the end of August, Maddy is in Walmart to buy some maternity pants. She has almost reached the area of the store she wants when she sees Anderson walking by. She turns around, holds still. It's unlikely he saw her, it was just a flash of him that she saw. But no, he did see her. She hears him behind her. "Maddy."

She turns to face him. He lifts his chin in that casual and dismissive way, his greeting. She says nothing.

"Well, look who's here," he says.

"I thought it was your day off."

"It is. I came in for some dude that had to go to a funeral. Guess that gets you pretty excited, huh? What with your love affair with cemeteries."

"I have a lot to do, Anderson, so . . ."

He leans against the shelf, blocking her way. He's trying to be sexy, crossing his arms to display his muscles, but she doesn't care anymore.

"Come on now," he says. "You've got time for a Coke, right? I'll buy you some French fries, too."

"Actually, no, I don't have time."

"I went over to your house the other day," he says. "I sat outside for the longest time. I figured you'd see me and come out. I waited a long time, for nothing."

Before, she would have apologized to him. Now she does not.

He looks around, then leans in. "I wanted to see you bad, you know what I mean?"

She snorts.

"I did, I swear! Look, I know I said some things."

"Yes. Like you want nothing to do with me and I'm crazy."

"Okay, I was a jerk. But you know, it was a big surprise, what you told me. I was, like, in shock, okay?" He scans her body. "So are you still?"

"Am I still what?"

He shrugs. "You know, pregnant?" It's as if the word is a cut in his mouth that he has to speak around.

It occurs to her to say *None of your business*, which, so far as she is concerned, is true. But what she really wants is to get rid of him, and so she says, "Yes, I am still pregnant. The baby is due on Christmas Day."

His face softens. "Awwwwww."

Now she's confused, and a little frightened. "I have to go," she says, and starts to walk away.

He takes her arm. "I'll come and see you tonight," he says. "About eight o'clock."

Great. Then her dad will tell him where she is. Unless she warns her dad not to. In which case, her dad will get all upset, and anything can happen.

"I don't live there anymore."

"Where do you live?"

THE STORY OF ARTHUR TRULUV

"None of your business."

He smiles. "What, do you live with that old dude that goes to visit his wife every day? That fucking lecher you told me about?"

She moves closer to him.

"Let me tell you something, Anderson. You could live to be a thousand years old and never begin to measure up to the kind of man Arthur Moses is. You can't see the broad side of a barn for your ego. I wish I'd never met you."

"Yeah, well, you're having my baby, so . . ."

"It's not yours!" She bores her eyes into his.

"Are you fucking kidding me? You said it was mine!"

"I guess we both said things that aren't true, didn't we?"

She walks away, hopeful that he won't follow her, and he doesn't.

It's later than Maddy thought it would be when she gets home. She went to Goodwill for clothes and had the good luck to find not only a great pair of maternity jeans but a top that wasn't hideous. And she found a child's book on trees that she bought for the baby. It's hard to think that what's growing inside her will someday be a fully formed little kid who can listen to books, then read them himself, but it's true. It's also hard to remember that the baby is half Anderson. But the way she looks at it most times is that mostly the baby is itself, a blank slate, and she will do everything she

can to make sure her child does not have the isolating experience growing up that she did. All the while she lived with
her father, she felt like a rope unraveling.

"Arthur?" she calls, coming in the front door. No answer.
"Hello?"

They must have gone out somewhere, but not for long:
she smells dinner in the oven. She takes a peek and sees a
chicken roasting, potatoes baking. On the counter, a perfect-
looking pie, cherry crumb-topped, she guesses, judging by
the dark red juice that has bubbled out of the crust.

She goes upstairs and puts away her clothes, then puts
the little book on her bookshelf. She'll show it to Arthur and
ask him what he thinks. He's the nature expert.

On her desk are the Hamburgers and the photo of her
mother, but now she sees something different, too. A pretty
silver picture frame, maybe eight by ten, and in it is another
picture of her mother. Or no, it's the same picture, but it has
been restored. The image is much clearer. Maddy picks up
the frame and stares into her mother's face, that smiling,
confident, happy face, sure of a future she never got to have.

Where did this photo come from?

Well, it can only have come from Arthur or Lucille. The
cat didn't do it. Or . . . her father? No. It was Arthur.

She sits in the desk chair holding the photo, a bit over-
whelmed. In many respects, sorrow and disappointment are
easier for her to handle than this outpouring of attention
and affection that she has been offered by these two old people. It's odd, it's just so odd, all that has happened to her.
Trying to separate the events in order to determine what led

to what is like trying to distinguish the beginning and end of one strand of spaghetti on a platter piled high with the pasta. If she hadn't had the home life she did, would she have had a better time at school? If she had had a better time at school, would she have ever met Arthur? Would she be going to art school without the intervention of Mr. Lyons? If she hadn't lived here, would she ever have come to such an appreciation of what old people offer?

She hears Arthur and Lucille come in. She goes downstairs to meet them.

"There she is!" Lucille says, as though they've been out looking for her. But where they have been, Maddy sees, is to Willigan's for ice cream: Arthur is holding the polka-dot bag.

"Thank you for that picture of my mom," Maddy says, and she minds very much the fact that her throat tightens. Maddy supposes it will never go away, the wrenching feeling that comes to her when she thinks about her mother.

"It was Lucille's idea," Arthur says.

"No, it was my idea to get a big picture made of *Frank*," Lucille says. "Which I did. I cut one of him out of the yearbook to get made into an eight-by-ten. He's wearing his letter sweater and he looks so handsome. What a dish he was. Then Arthur said why didn't we do the same thing with that terrible, beat-up photo of your mom?"

"Well," Maddy says. "Thank you both."

"Are you hungry?" Lucille asks. Her favorite thing is asking that and having you say yes. And then after you say yes, she recites what the menu will be. And then when she serves it to you, she recites it again. She lays the meat on your plate and says, "Now. There's a nice piece of *chicken*."

"I am hungry," Maddy says.

"Well, you two go and wash up and I'll have everything on the table before you get back. We're having baked chicken stuffed with dressing made with fresh rosemary, sage, and thyme; and twice-baked potatoes with butter and sour cream; and a Caesar salad, but I'll coddle the egg on account of the baby. And Martha Washington's cherry pie with Willigan's French vanilla ice cream."

One afternoon in September when Arthur is off at the cemetery, Maddy takes a break from cleaning and goes up into her room. She is sitting at her desk with her candy box when Lucille barges in.

"Cranberry nut bars!" she says, holding out a plate with several treats arranged on one of her paper doilies. "I made up a kind of orange glaze to put on them, and it is the most delicious thing!" Then, seeing that Maddy has her hand over the box, she says, "Oh. Am I disturbing you?"

"I guess I think people should knock," Maddy says. "Before entering someone's private space."

Lucille's exuberance drains from her face.

"It's okay," Maddy says, pushing the box off to the side. "But maybe in the future . . ."

"Oh, I hear you," Lucille says. "Loud and clear. You want your privacy."

She gestures with the plate toward the candy box. "What's that?"

Maddy has to laugh. "Well, Lucille, what that is, is private."

Lucille stands there, then asks, "So, would you like me to leave you the bars?"

"Yeah, all right," Maddy says.

"And how about if I bring you some milk? You need your milk."

"I'll get it later," Maddy says.

"You might as well have it now. Eating these will make you thirsty." Lucille puts the plate down on Maddy's desk and peers into the candy box.

"Is that dollhouse furniture in there?"

Maddy sighs. Then she attempts a glare at Lucille that turns to tears filling her eyes. When people talk about pregnancy making you emotional, they're not kidding.

"Yes. That's not all that's in there. But there is some dollhouse furniture."

And then, when Lucille's face softens and she falls silent, Maddy pushes the box toward her. Let her know about the pearl ring, the faded length of blue ribbon. Things she has scavenged.

"Ohhhh," Lucille says softly. "I had dollhouse furniture like that. Can I see it?"

Maddy takes out the bed, the sofa, the armchair.

"Look at that," Lucille says, her hands clasped beneath her chin. "Did you used to play with that, when you were little?"

Maddy shrugs. "It was my mom's. I guess there used to be more. But this was all I ever found."

"I played with my dollhouse all the time," Lucille says. "Oh, I just loved it! I thought, this is exactly how I'm going to live. I'm going to have a house full of sunshine and every room will be beautiful!

"I would arrange things in the house just so. I made lace curtains for all the windows, and I cut out squares of fabric to be bedspreads. I made little tiny pillows; my mother was a wonderful seamstress and she helped me. And do you know, every time I knelt before that house and peered into it, it was as though I was living there already, it was like everything I wanted had come true in the future and life was just waiting for me to catch up to it. I thought that house the happiest place, the most complete, and . . . Well. It was just pretend, wasn't it? It was a child's dream. And I was a foolish child and I guess I turned into a foolish old woman."

Her head falls, her hands, and a great quiet descends in the room.

Then Maddy says, "Sometimes when I take out the furniture, I can almost feel her there. My mother. And I can feel what she must have been like. I . . . Well, I arrange things, too; I know it's only three things, but I arrange what I've got and then I imagine the rest. I used to make houses everywhere when I was a little girl: outside under the bushes, in shoe boxes that I kept hidden in my closet. I used my mom's dollhouse furniture and then I would cut things out of magazines. Furniture, rugs, even things for outside the house: trees, flowers, bushes. Birds. I would make these little houses and I would pretend I lived there with my mother. And we were so happy."

Lucille hesitates, then reaches over to put her hand on top of Maddy's head.

"You know what?" she says.

"What."

"Some things come true. They might come true in ways different than we might have predicted, but some things do come true."

Maddy looks up, directly into those pale blue eyes, sad and joyful, joyful and sad. "Lucille?"

"Yes?"

"How about we go down to the kitchen and have those bars?"

Lucille puffs herself up. "Well, I thought you'd never ask."

After dinner, they are sitting on the porch coming up with suggestions for names for the baby. But this is an exhausting enterprise, and soon the conversation drifts to whether or not Lucille should sell her house. The real estate agent, having said she didn't want to pressure her, is pressuring her. There is a call almost every other day, now coming to Arthur's house, and Arthur often has a pleasant little chat with Rhonda before he calls Lucille to the phone. Lucille told Maddy that she thinks he and the realtor have gotten a bit too cozy. "She's a brash one, that Rhonda," Lucille said. "A real hussy. Those big-bosomed women have such a sense of entitlement; I have always said that. I hate to cooperate with her, but she is the top-rated realtor, she'll get me the best price. I might as well sell before the winter sets in. I guess she's right."

But, "You don't *have* to sell, Lucille," Arthur says now. "Don't let Rhonda make you do something you're not ready for."

Maddy thinks she can see Lucille bristle at Arthur using Rhonda's name. It's her opinion that Lucille is jealous; Rhonda, whom she has met, is actually a very nice person, and Arthur will have a pleasant chat with anyone who calls, even a wrong number.

"But that's just it," Lucille says. "I might be ready."

"You can take a little time," Arthur says, and Lucille falls abruptly silent.

Then, "If you prefer, Arthur," she says. "I can move into some *apartment*."

"You're fine here," Arthur says. "Everything is working out."

"But I've only been here for a few weeks. Who knows how you'll feel after . . ."

"Everything is fine!" Arthur says. "You're happy here, aren't you? And we're happy to have you, aren't we, Maddy?"

"Totally!" Maddy says.

"Well, all right then," Lucille says. "All right."

They sit for a while, thinking their separate thoughts, watching the evening come. The clouds pinken and the roosting birds grow quiet; lights go on in houses. And then Lucille says, "You know, I just had a realization about that. About happiness, I mean. Today, when you people were out, I came out to sit on the porch, and I looked over at my porch. My old porch. And the old porch made me sad, because it was all about my life over there, which was mostly awful. Oh, I pretended it was all right—even to myself, I pretended— but it was mostly awful. And here, I've been so much happier. So I was sitting here and thinking that, and I had the funniest thought, which was that happiness was sitting with me." She points to the chair Maddy is in. "It was sitting right there, like it was a person or something. I swear I could feel its presence, like when you don't look at another person, but you're seeing them anyway. Do you know what I mean?"

"'Course I do," Arthur says. "I do it every day in the cemetery."

Maddy says nothing, but she's thinking, *I do it with my mom.*

"Well, anyway," Lucille says, "I felt like some embodiment of happiness was sitting there, and I was afraid to look over at it. I was afraid it would go away. And then it talked. The happiness, it talked, it said, 'Look at me.' So I looked over. And happiness said, 'You're not looking at me. You're looking at you.'"

"What does that mean?" Arthur asks.

"Well, just that it's all up to us, isn't it?"

Arthur says, "You know, I think teaching has been good for you, Lucille."

"And you really don't mind having the students come here?"

"At this point," Arthur says, "you might as well bring in the Russian Army."

"But . . . you mean that in the good way, right?" Lucille says.

"I mean that in the best way," says Arthur.

Lucille turns to Maddy. "I wonder something. And I'm just going to say it. Would you ever consider naming the baby Emma Jean?"

"If it's a girl?"

"Oh, it's a girl. I know it is. You ask them to tell you, you'll see."

"I don't want to know," Maddy says. "I want to be surprised."

"I just don't understand that," Lucille says. "I would want to know!"

"And I want to be surprised."

"Well, it's no surprise anyway, because I know it's a girl. I'm doing the whole layette in pink."

"Great!" Maddy says. "Boys can wear pink."

Lucille says nothing, and Arthur scratches his head.

"It's a whole new world," Maddy says, smiling.

A squirrel races across the lawn in front of them, cheeks fat with bounty.

Lucille shudders. "Rodents!" she says. "Rodents with bushy tails."

They watch the squirrel dig down to its elbows, a hole so deep its head disappears. Then it takes the nut from its mouth, uses its nose to nudge it into the hole, and quickly covers it back up.

Lucille laughs. "They're kind of fun to watch, aren't they? Do you know, I have never taken the time."

"Sometimes you see them swinging through the trees like acrobats," Arthur says. "I always like to watch that."

"Their tails help them balance," Maddy says.

Arthur smiles over at her. "That's right!"

"How do they ever find where they buried those things?" Lucille asks. "The walnuts. I suppose they just steal from each other."

"Acorns, I think you mean," Arthur says. "Red-oak acorns, mostly; they like those better than white-oak acorns. And they lick them before they bury them, and that's how they find them later, by their own scent; they can smell it even under snow."

"What if all you could eat is one food?" Lucille asks. "Wouldn't that be awful?"

"They eat more than nuts," Arthur says. "They eat leaves and seeds and insect eggs, even birds' eggs, I'm sorry to say. Worse than that, they eat spring flowers!"

"They chew on bones, too," Maddy says. "For the calcium. And they lick the salt on the roads in wintertime."

"Well, aren't you two just the Nature Channel," Lucille says.

As they watch, the squirrel runs into the street and is narrowly missed by an oncoming car. Maddy breathes out a sigh of relief; she can't stand to see anything killed. Beyond her tenderheartedness toward animals, there is something else that happens whenever she sees that. Some sense of futility about life comes over her, some dark memory gets stirred.

A car pulls up next to the curb, and a man gets out. In the dim light, it's hard to see who it might be. But then Maddy jumps to her feet. "No!" she says.

Arthur, confused, stands up. "What is it?" he asks.

Maddy ignores him. Instead, she leans over the railing of the porch to shout, "Don't come up here! Go away!"

"Who is that?" Lucille asks Arthur.

"Beats me," Arthur says.

Maddy goes down the steps and halfway down the walk. "Go home, Anderson. I don't want to see you anymore."

"You wouldn't have told me that old man's name unless you wanted me to come," he says. "You probably want me to rescue you or some romantic shit. Well, here I am."

"I don't want you to *rescue* me. I don't need rescuing. And I told you, I don't want to see you anymore."

"Bullshit."

From the porch, Arthur calls, "Who is that? Are you all right, Maddy?" He and Lucille are standing at the railing, peering out.

Anderson looks over at the house. "Jesus Christ. This is who you're living with?"

Maddy lowers her voice. "Please leave, Anderson. I don't want you here. I'll call you later. We can talk about this. I don't want you here."

She tries to take his arm and pull him toward the car, but

he yanks away roughly, knocking her off balance, and she nearly falls.

"Maddy!" Arthur calls.

She takes Anderson's arm again. "If you don't go, I'm going to call the cops."

"Fuck you, Maddy, the cops won't do anything. I'm not doing anything!"

"Young man?" she hears from the porch. It's Arthur, standing at the top of the stairs with a baseball bat.

Anderson's expression changes. "Really?" he asks, grinning.

"Really," Arthur says, and starts walking slowly toward him.

Anderson's hands curl into fists. "Better take it easy, old man."

Now Arthur picks up the pace while Maddy stands terrified on the lawn.

"Oh, for fuck's sake, I'm going, okay?" Anderson says, but apparently he isn't moving fast enough for Arthur, who has increased his own speed.

Anderson jumps in the car and screeches away from the curb. And Arthur starts to run after him. He runs! He may be an old man, but look at him go.

Suddenly, then, Arthur stops. He bends over, his hands on his knees. Maddy catches up to him. "Are you okay? Arthur?"

Arthur's breathing is rapid, but he is jubilant. "Are *you* okay?" he asks, and she nods.

"What is going *on*?" Lucille yells from the porch. Maddy sees that a few other people are looking out their windows.

"Everything's fine," Arthur yells. "It's all over, folks." And then, to Maddy, "Whew! I believe I'll have another piece of pie. How about you?"

Before she goes to bed, Maddy knocks on Arthur's bedroom door. He stays up for quite a while after he goes to bed, just thinking, he's told Maddy. An old habit, to run the day he's had past himself for review. "Come in!" he says, and she comes to stand by the bedside to show Arthur the book about trees that she bought for the baby.

Arthur takes it from her and pages through it carefully. "Well, it's a very nice book," he says, handing it back. "Not quite as inclusive as I'd like to see. But a very nice little book. It'll get him started."

"Don't you mean 'her'?"

"I'm *never* wrong about a baby's sex," Arthur says in a high voice. He's imitating Lucille, whom they can hear snoring from her room down the hall. "Or about anything *else*." Then, shrugging, he says, "You gotta love her."

"It must be wonderful to be so confident," Maddy says.

"I suppose it is." He looks up at her, his brown eyes huge behind his glasses. She'd never say this to him in case it would hurt his dignity, but he's so *cute*.

"Good night, Arthur," Maddy says.

She goes to her room and sits in the little pink chair with

her photography book. She studies each image carefully, rocking, with her hand on her stomach. There's so much she can't wait for.

The roses are gone, and September has passed. It was a lovely month, all of them sitting on the porch in the afternoons while it was still warm enough to watch the schoolchildren being disgorged from buses, then running toward home in zigzag patterns, smacking each other with backpacks, or strolling dreamily along.

Now it is a war of days: on Monday, you might need a jacket; on Tuesday, it might get warm enough for you to lie in the grass in shirtsleeves. Assuming you can still lie in the grass, which, alas, Arthur can no longer do. Nola was one for that: in Indian summer, she might abandon peeling potatoes to go out and lie in the grass to watch the clouds pass by. In her apron. He came home from work one day and there she was in the backyard, still holding the peeler, and when she saw Arthur, she pointed to the sky and said, "Look! Do you see the elephant?" And he sure enough did, and he told her so. The one to tell. The one to be told by. For him, that was marriage.

One day when Arthur and Maddy are out on the porch alone, he watches Maddy studying the children with a particular intensity. After a while, she turns to him and, with a kind of sadness, says, "I don't see how you can ever learn not to make mistakes with children."

Arthur is whittling a little bird for the ever-coming baby. He doesn't look up to answer. "I don't see how, either. Everybody makes mistakes, sometimes even before we get up in the morning. We can't help but make mistakes. The important thing is to keep trying. And to apologize when you need to."

Maddy tries to tuck her feet beneath her, but it's gotten too hard to do. Soon she won't be able to see her feet. She'll need help tying her shoes.

She watches Arthur whittle; there's a meditative comfort in it. He's talented at a lot of things he never talks about, and he's so generous, overly generous, Maddy thinks. You have to be careful about saying what you like around him; it will show up in your room the next day. When school started, Maddy said she had always loved pencil boxes, and the next day, one he had made from a cigar box was on her desk, full of sparkly pencils and a pink eraser. Not only that, he had made a little tiny pencil box for the baby, and in it was a pacifier (blue).

Halloween is almost upon them. On his way to bed one night, Arthur sees light coming from under Maddy's door. She's always rather quiet, but today she barely said a word. He supposes she might be worn out from making Halloween treats for the kids with Lucille. They made taffy apples, at least fifty of them, because Lucille would not accept the fact that parents wouldn't allow such treats any longer. Finally, by way of compromise, she attached a note to each apple, saying, THESE ARE NOT POISON. THEY WERE MADE BY LUCILLE HOWARD, MASTER BAKER. CALL 555-9986 IF ANY DOUBTS.

Lucille also asked Maddy to help her wrap Tootsie Pops in Kleenex to look like ghosts. The Kleenex was tied on with orange or black ribbon, and Maddy gave all the little ghosts ghoulish black eyes. Arthur helped for a while, but the repetitiveness got to him. He excused himself for the bathroom, then never came back. The women found him in the living room, snoring, Gordon asleep in his lap.

Now Arthur knocks on Maddy's door.

"Who is it?"

"Gordon," he says, and it's true; the cat is lying outside her door.

"Come in."

He opens the door and sees her sitting on her bed, back against the wall, a quilt Lucille made for her wrapped around her. She's holding something that she covers with the quilt as he approaches. Her big eyes are bigger than usual; she looks nervous. He wonders if that awful Anderson has been after her.

"Just wanted to see how you are today. Are you feeling all right?"

"Yeah. I guess."

"Anything I can do for you?"

"No." She swallows.

Gordon jumps up and lies next to her. He's on high alert, muscles tensed, his tail up and moving through the air in lazy S's. He's ready to pounce.

Arthur shifts on the chair. "I don't want to pry, Maddy, but has that boy been bothering you? That Anderson?"

"No." Her voice is so small.

"Is it . . . ?"

She bursts into tears. Arthur leaps to his feet, alarmed, and rushes to sit beside her. Gordon leaps off the bed and takes up another strategic position on Maddy's desk.

"Does anything hurt? Are you okay?"

"I'm okay," she says. "I'm just . . ." She looks over at the door. "Can we get a lock put on that door, do you think?"

"Of course. Is that it? Are you afraid of intruders?"

"No."

She picks at the quilt.

"Maddy?"

She looks up at him. "I don't want Lucille coming in here all the time. I like her, I really do, but I just need . . . She told me all about what will happen when I deliver and now I'm just so scared!"

"What did she say?"

Maddy begins to wail. "She said it would feel like my body was being torn in *half*!"

She wipes off her face, reddened now, and asks quietly, "Where is she? Do you think she can hear us?"

"She's asleep, I heard her sawing logs when I went past her room. Lord, that woman could be her own percussion section in the St. Louis Symphony Orchestra."

Maddy laughs, in spite of herself.

"I'm not sure how much Lucille knows about childbirth," Arthur says. "She's never had a baby."

"I know, but she's talked to a lot of people who have."

"So have I!"

"Really?"

"Well, I've talked to a few. Mostly the women . . . you know . . . Mostly that's women's conversation. But I'll tell you one thing. This one woman I knew, friend of Nola's, she had her baby in half an hour. Came out of her like a greased cannonball."

"That wasn't her first."

"No. But how did you know that?"

Maddy pulls the book she's been hiding out from under the quilt.

It's a battered tome called *You and Your Delivery, and Beyond*. "It says in here that the first delivery lasts the longest. That's what everything I googled said, too. And there's all this stuff about if you want medicine or if you don't and why you should do this and why you shouldn't do that and the stages of labor and how you're supposed to breathe and I don't get it! I don't want to hurt the baby but I don't know what they're *talking* about, I tried it and I don't know if it's right, I don't know anything and I just want . . ." Now she begins to cry again. "I just want my *mother*." She covers her face and weeps, rocking back and forth, back and forth.

Arthur nods, his throat tight.

"Well, you did sign up for those classes, right? The Amaze classes?"

She sniffs. "Lamaze."

"Lamaze, that's it!" He pooches his lips out. "Lamaze. What does that mean?"

Maddy shrugs. "*I* don't know. But I don't start that for another few weeks and I don't even have anyone to go with me. Everyone else will have their husbands and I have to go alone like a loser."

"No, you don't," Arthur says.

She looks at him.

"I'll go with you."

"You don't have to do that. No, Truluv. I can do it. I'm just . . ."

"Well, just saying. If you don't want to go alone, I'll go, too. Might be kind of interesting!"

"That's so nice of you. But see, you have to get on the floor."

"*I* have to get on the floor? Why do I have to get on the floor?"

"Because the helper? He—or she—gets behind the pregnant woman and helps her. I don't know. I've only seen pictures."

"Well, I could bring my fold-up chair and maybe do it from there?"

"I don't know."

"All right. I'll tell you what. I'll just go with you to the first class. I'll say I'm your grandfather. Okay? We'll just go together and see what's what. Then you can decide if you want me to come anymore. My schedule is wide open. Except at noon. So I'll come any other time you want."

"Okay. The classes are in the evening. But we won't say you're my grandfather. We'll say you're my friend."

"Even better." He stands up to relieve some pressure on his back. He points to the book. "Where'd you get that?"

"Goodwill."

"Looks kind of old."

"I guess. I go to the library and google stuff, too, but I like the books. I like to take my time and I like the old pictures. All the moms look so pretty, seems like they all have these beautiful ribbons in their hair. I have a lot more books."

Arthur looks around the room. "Where?"

Maddy climbs out of bed and goes to the closet, opens it. There are stacks and stacks of books in there. He moves closer to inspect them: books on labor and delivery. Books on pregnancy, week by week. On top of one stack is a book about what your baby would ask for if he or she could talk. That looks interesting. Arthur picks it up. "Have you read this one?"

She nods.

"Any good?"

"I guess. Did you know that the baby can hear music when he's inside?"

"Is that right?"

"Yes."

Arthur lowers his voice to a whisper. "Can he hear us talking right now?"

"That's what they say. And he can suck his thumb. And after they're born, when they start to reach for things, they try to catch light. They close their fist around it, and they think they have it in their hands. Isn't that cool? They like to be talked to and sung to. And sometimes they want to be cuddled—you wrap them like a papoose, and I did learn how to do that—but other times they want to be alone, like they just want to think their own thoughts. That's what I read somewhere."

"Huh." Arthur walks over to the window and looks out. The moon is full, some of the trees look silver-tipped. He turns and regards Maddy, who seems to him at this moment like nothing more than a wee thing in a nest. "I would like to ask a favor, Maddy."

"Okay."

"I can't participate in this like your mother would. But here's what I can do. I can listen. I can learn with you. I can go to the doctor with you, if you'd like. I'll wait in the lobby on the day he's born and I'll be the second to welcome him wholeheartedly into the world."

"Maybe the third," Maddy says ruefully. "Lucille already made her reservation."

"Well," Arthur says. "This is one time when she will not be in charge. Okay? You're in charge."

She looks up at him.

Arthur points to her. "You're the one!"

"Okay!"

"You all right now?" Arthur asks. "Think you can sleep?"

"Yes. Thank you."

Arthur flips through the book on what babies would ask. "There's a lot of nice pictures in here of the little fellows."

"And girls," Maddy says.

"Of course. Would you mind if I borrow this? I finished my Western, I'm plumb out of something good to read."

"Sure, take it."

"I might have some questions for you after I look at it."

"Okay."

She lies down, pulls the blanket up. "Would you turn out the light, Truluv?"

He does so, then makes his way to his room. He prepares for bed quickly so he can get under the covers and see what she's been seeing, and then talk to her about it. He'll also talk to Lucille.

To learn that someone living in the same house with you has been feeling so alone and you didn't even know!

The leaves turn and because there is so little rain, they are on the trees even in November. It's glorious, Arthur thinks. It's so beautiful that every time he looks outside, it hurts in his chest. Some leaves are a bright yellow, some a deep red, some coral-colored, and some are little stained-glass windows of many colors all on one leaf. Lucille ironed some leaves between wax paper and hung them in the kitchen window. It was something she used to do with her fourth graders. "Kids probably only look at leaves *online* now," she grumbled, while she ironed them.

She's begun to make all kinds of crafty things, place mats and napkins and pillowcases and lots of things for the baby. Things to sleep in, things to lie on, things to lie under.

Mostly in pink. Arthur did feel a pang the first time he heard the sewing machine running, but he likes it now, that sound of domestic industry. He likes domestics, period. As a spectator sport. He likes to watch the women fold towels in front of *Dancing with the Stars*. He likes the pile of freshly laundered and folded T-shirts and shorts and socks that gets left at the foot of his bed once a week, and the way his shirts and pants are taken out of the dryer damp and immediately put on hangers, so there's not a single wrinkle in them. He likes the scent of the lemon oil Maddy uses on the wood, he likes how the bathroom sparkles. Lucille has outlawed all the cleaning products that he used to use (not that he used them all that much, but he had them, that has to count for something!). It's all organic now, or nontoxic or gluten-free or manna from heaven or whatever, Arthur isn't sure what those two go off and buy or where they buy it. But it doesn't matter. The house practically purrs. And wonder of wonders, both Maddy and Lucille leave the toilet seat up most of the time.

Lucille has been making nourishing soups and stews, and yesterday she made caramel rolls that smelled so good Arthur complained that she was going to put him into heart failure with just the smell alone. "They're not for you, they're the demo for my class," she told him, but that's what she always tells him when she makes things for her classes, and then she always saves some for him and for Maddy. And for herself. Always. Every morning after she's taught a class, there's some treat left on her special blue platter in the middle of the kitchen table. "I'm getting *fat*," Maddy frequently complains, and both Arthur and Lucille always respond in unison: "You're *supposed* to!"

This morning, while Lucille busily (and noisily!) sets up for teaching her class how to make a braided poppy seed egg bread, Arthur goes to the cemetery for an early lunch with Nola. It's a bit chilly out, but the sun is warm; it's the kind of weather that makes for a simultaneous feeling of gratitude and wariness, what with winter not far away, big puffy overcoats crowding the racks in the stores.

He heads, as if being directed, to a row of graves far from Nola's and goes to the last plot, the one by the fence, close to the sounds of traffic. The cheap seats, he supposes. He always feels a little sorry for people buried in such places, as though they're aware. Maybe they are aware. But if they are, he thinks they've moved beyond status or comparison or bitterness. If they are aware, they just . . . Well, they just are, and they are filled with their areness. Is how he thinks of it.

The grave at the end has a stone with an angel carved into it. She's meant to be a kind of guardian angel, Arthur thinks, wings at rest, hands clasped, her gaze focused downward. He moves closer and squints at the name: *James Linten. Born February 17, 1970. Died January 3, 2003.*

Well. Another youngster. Cancer? he wonders. But no, here it comes: *A car wreck; he slid on black ice. Last thing he did was try to change the radio station. And as soon as the car began to slide, he knew. Right into the path of a truck. He knew that he would die and in the remarkable way that these things happen, he got ready. He was ready.*

Arthur stands with his hat in one hand, his chair in the

other. And then, though he has never done this before, he opens his chair and sits beside the grave of someone other than Nola. *He was ready.*

Arthur has had friends die, he has visited them in hospitals near the end, and always he saw something when people were ready: a gentle turning-away-from. And what he always hoped was that in turning away, they were also turning toward. For everything there truly is a season; if his life's work has not taught him that, it has taught him nothing. The birth of spring, the fullness of summer, the push of glory in the fall, the quiet of winter.

James Linten. Thirty-two years old. Father of twins.

Arthur stands and folds up his chair. He'd rather not think of those twins, whom he thinks must have embraced their father's legs when he came in the door. James may have been ready; he doubts those twins were. And then he has to laugh at himself, at the realness of his imagination. Still, he looks over his shoulder as he walks away, and there is *something*.

He wanders a bit more. There's the stone dog lying at the base of Benjamin Spencer's headstone that he's seen many times, muzzle on its paws. There's a drawing of a turkey on Frieda Loney's grave, the kind children make from their hands. There's a carved weeping woman draped over Beth Ann King's black granite marker that he does not like to look at.

He walks past Susan James: *Died on vacation in a water-skiing accident, the clouds in a blue summer sky the last thing she saw.* Here is Henry Wilcox, *Lived 101 years out of pure stubbornness. Would never take his pocket watch off except when he bathed, and even then the watch was left on the closed lid of the toilet so he could keep an eye on it. No one ever knew why it was so important to him. "That's my business," he always said. Died in a car crash that was not his fault; he'd been on the way to get a proper shave.* Bruce Hudson: *Died at forty-five from a concussion, after a fistfight that began when a joke wasn't so funny.*

"Nola," Arthur says when, out of breath, he reaches her grave at last. He settles down in his chair. "A nice day, but winter's sticking its nose out the door." And then he says nothing, just sits and enjoys the sun and the sky and the mild scent of the damp earth.

In winter, Nola had to have flowers. She bought inexpensive bouquets at the florist's every week or so. Once she had one at the center of the kitchen table and the blossoms from the flowers had begun to fall, there was a ring of petals at the foot of the vase. At breakfast one day, Arthur cleaned them up and rearranged the stems. Nola sat watching him. Then she said, "What are you doing?"

"What?" he said. "They're dying."

"They're still beautiful," she said, "the petals, loose like that. Please don't clean them up. The falling . . . it's just part of it. I bring buds home, the blossoms open up, the petals fall, and I like all of it."

At one o'clock, Arthur is going with Maddy to her obstetrician's office. She told him it might be fun for him to hear the baby's heartbeat, but Arthur suspects she has an ulterior motive. She and Lucille both have been badgering him to go to a doctor for his waning appetite, his declining strength, for the pains he's been having in his stomach, and for the way he seems to need so much more sleep lately. The women can't count on him to chime in on anything they watch on television anymore; they tell him they look over at him to tell him something and he's gone, his head tilted oddly, his mouth agape. The only one who doesn't bother him about this is Gordon, although, come to think of it, the cat does his own kind of surveillance: he rarely leaves Arthur's side and he sleeps on his bed all night, every night.

Maddy probably figures that if her OB meets Arthur, he will, based on his appearance alone, advise Arthur to go and get a checkup. "The baby's doing well!" he imagines Dr. Hunter saying. "But you, Arthur, you don't look so good. When's the last time you had some lab work done?"

But here's the thing. Arthur is finished with doctors. There is something that has come upon him that he can't quite explain. He is not disaffected or depressed; if anything, it's quite the opposite. He has a lively and interesting home, full of love and laughter. He and Lucille and Maddy are like a modernized, downsized version of *The Waltons*, what with the way they all say good night to each other, every night. He looks forward to life as much as he ever did. But going to doctors? He is done with that. He's an old man living an old man's life. He thinks of himself as a caboose on a long, long train. The engine is close to the terminal; but the caboose is far from it. He's all right. He's Nola's blossoms, and he's ready.

As he and Maddy are ushered into the doctor's office, Dr. Hunter rushes over to him. "How are *you*, sir!" he says, and shakes Arthur's hand, looking obliquely into his eyes, probably at the yellowish color that has appeared in his sclera. Arthur mostly views this as a trick of the light, nothing to worry about.

"Hundred percent," Arthur says. "And you?"

"Oh, just great," the doctor says, and turns to Maddy. They have a conversation Arthur can't quite hear, and then Dr. Hunter smears some goo on Maddy's belly, and moves something that looks like a microphone around on it. Arthur nearly jumps out of his chair when he hears a loud, rhythmic whooshing sound.

"Hear it?" Dr. Hunter asks, smiling.

Arthur stares at him. "But is that . . . Is that the *baby*?"

"That's the baby's heart."

"Is there something wrong?"

"No!" says Dr. Hunter. "Don't you hear how strong that beat is?"

"Yes, but the loudness! It's so loud!"

"Well," Dr. Hunter says. "It's amplified."

"Even so," Arthur says. "Must be a boy in there."

"Fifty percent chance," says Dr. Hunter, all smug-looking. He knows then, Arthur thinks. He tries to catch the doctor's eye and wink at him, but Dr. Hunter is looking at

Maddy now. Just as well. What would a wink mean, any-way? Well, it would mean that it was a boy. Who just might be called Arthur, you never know.

Two days before Thanksgiving, Maddy is coming back from having visited with the administration at the school she will be attending in the spring. It is still something she can't quite realize, that she'll be living in a dorm with her baby and her roommate, who will be another single mother, and attending classes. She was shown the dorm rooms, as well as the daycare center where her baby would be while she was in class. She saw the library, the gleaming wooden tables where she could go and study. She was told that free babysit-ting would be provided twice a week by students at the col-lege, and that she herself would meet with the director of the program once a month just to be sure that she was doing all right with grades and with adjustment. One thing Mad-dy's sure of is that she'll be doing all right with grades. She can't wait to get into that library.

As the bus nears the station, she lets go of the fantasy she was enjoying: herself in her dorm room in warm pajamas, snow falling, her baby sleeping and her with a textbook about photography on her lap. The only thing that isn't paid for is books, and Arthur wants to pay for that, but Maddy won't let him. She'll have no trouble buying her own books. She's saving money like crazy.

Before she goes home, Maddy will stop at the library to

check out some movies. She used one of her paychecks to modernize the TV, and she likes to watch old movies with Arthur and Lucille. She likes the backgrounds even more than the main stories: the clothes, the telephones, the cars, the music, the dancing. She likes the language: *Say! Gee, that's swell!* She loves the soft-focus shooting of the women, especially in their close-ups. (Gloria Swanson, with her grimacing smile and crazy-wide eyes: *All right, Mr. DeMille, I'm ready for my close-up.*)

Of course, Arthur and Lucille are her own personal handbook of archaic terms. She loves living with them and she loves them. Whenever she thinks this, that she loves them, there is a kind of momentary internal paralysis, a fear of being truly inside the words she's thinking. But she is.

The other night, they ate the popcorn balls Lucille had made and watched *Pennies from Heaven*. Maddy, curled under a pink crocheted afghan, was struck by the lyrics of the song; the idea of happiness being payment for having endured adversity. Maddy's life lately has been an onslaught of outsize good fortune. Deep inside is a voice wanting to taunt her, to tell her she is undeserving of it, to not trust it because it won't last, good things never last. Or it tells her she will fuck up and lose everything. But she's gotten better at tuning that voice out.

She gets off the bus and starts the walk to the library. The baby is moving inside and Maddy puts her hand reflexively to her side to feel the kicks. She is talking to the baby as she walks along, as she often does, when she sees Anderson's car pull up to a stoplight. She stops walking. He doesn't see her, but there he is, with a blond-headed woman he now leans over to kiss. Maddy can taste that kiss. She stands watching, her hand still pressing against her side, and the baby goes quiet, as though it, too, is watching. Despite everything, despite *everything*, she suddenly feels an awful longing to be back with him. It makes no sense. But inside, it's as though her heart has been lassoed and is being gently tugged. For the first time, she is embarrassed about her big stomach. Her hand falls from her side.

She doesn't have a boyfriend anymore, and she's not sure she ever will again. Absurd to say that, perhaps; she's young. But she has a child soon to be born. It makes things complicated.

And then, as the light changes and Anderson's car takes off, she smiles again, because she is going home.

Arthur comes into the kitchen to find Lucille happily frantic. She's sitting at the table finalizing the Thanksgiving Day menu.

"I have fourteen dishes planned so far," she tells Arthur breathlessly, after he pours his coffee and sits down.

And then, when Arthur's response is only a kind of start, she waves her hand. "Don't worry, one dish is just cranberry-orange sauce, one is plain cranberry sauce, one is Parker House rolls, and four are desserts. It might be a bit much for just the three of us, but what's better than Thanksgiving leftovers?"

"Nothing!" Arthur says, feeling a bit like a dog sitting up for his biscuit, but he's thinking that's going to be an awful lot of food. Good Lord, he eats less than Gordon lately. "Do you think maybe we should invite somebody?" he asks.

Lucille looks at him, frowning. "Who?"

Arthur can't think of anyone. Seems like all of his friends are dead. Finally, "The mailman?" he asks.

"Oh, Arthur," Lucille says. "Now you've gone and made me sad, thinking about how there's nobody we can invite to Thanksgiving dinner."

"Why can't we invite the mailman?"

She drops her hand onto her pile of cookbooks. "You can't just invite anyone! We don't even know the mailman! Who *is* the mailman?"

"Well, he's a real nice fellow," Arthur says. "You know him! He's tall, slender. Red hair. He's got a beard. His name is . . . Eddie! That's it! His name is Eddie."

Now Lucille crosses her arms over her chest and regards him. "Eddie who? What's his last name?"

Arthur looks down and stirs his coffee.

Lucille pats his hand. "I think it's very sweet that you want to ask someone, Arthur. It's a nice impulse. But it's too late to do that now. People have made their plans."

"What about people who take your classes?"

"Arthur."

"What?"

She sighs.

"*What?*" Arthur asks.

"When you're a teacher—and remember, I say this from

experience—when you're a teacher, you have to maintain a professional distance. Okay? Remember when you were a kid and you never wanted to see your teacher in a bathroom? Well, it's still like that. I can't have my students over here all involved in my personal life. It would be breaking the fourth wall!"

Arthur looks around. "What fourth wall?"

"Ha ha. You know exactly what I mean."

"Well," Arthur says, "I still think we could find *some*one to invite. What about Maddy's father?"

"Are you kidding?" Lucille's eyes narrow and she leans in closer to speak quietly. "He's not such a nice person, you know. He certainly wasn't very nice to Maddy. Why do you think she's living with us? That poor girl. No. I don't think we should invite her father."

"Maybe we should ask Maddy," Arthur says.

Maddy comes into the kitchen, all dressed for the day, bright red sweater, black corduroy pants. She's the prettiest thing. Lucille says Maddy looks just like Ava Gardner, and the girl does bear a slight resemblance. "Ask me what?" she says.

"Nothing," Lucille says, but at the same time Arthur asks loudly, "Would you like to invite your father for Thanksgiving?"

"Arthur!" Lucille says, drawing back from her pile of cookbooks and in the process knocking one down onto the floor.

"I've got it," Maddy says, and hands the book to Lucille.

And then, to Arthur, "Yes, I would like to invite my dad. If it's okay."

"Well, of *course* it's okay," Lucille says, and Arthur has to work hard not to roll his eyes. "Does he like turkey?"

What a question, Arthur thinks. Who doesn't like turkey? It would be like not liking water. Though, knowing Lucille, if she gets any sense that the man might not like turkey, she'll do something like go out and buy a prime rib. She says she'll never spend all the money she'll get for her house before she dies, but at the rate she's going, Arthur's not so sure. He was worried she might have regrets about selling, but the only time she looks over at her house is to make comments about what the new people might do. Yesterday, she was in the kitchen laying out ingredients for her monkey bread class and she glanced over at her house and said, "I hope whoever moves in has the good sense not to put shutters anywhere."

"I *think* my dad likes turkey," Maddy says, and Lucille and Arthur look at each other.

Arthur suspects that neither he nor Lucille will ask Maddy if she never had Thanksgiving dinner. It can't be true that they didn't go to *some*one's house for the holiday. Or out to some restaurant. If it is true, he doesn't want to know.

But then Maddy says, "We always had Chinese on Thanksgiving. On all the holidays, actually. I know he likes chicken and duck. So he must like turkey."

"I'll get a duck, too," Lucille says. But then Maddy and

Arthur both say, *"No!"* and she says, "All *right*! I had no idea where I was going to get one anyway."

"Tell him to come at four in the afternoon," Lucille says. And though her lips are pinched tightly together, she attempts a smile. Arthur can't help it; he thinks she looks constipated.

"Well, this is just fine!" Arthur says. "I'll get some wood and we'll build a fire that day."

"I'll get a wreath for the door," Maddy says.

Gordon, sitting next to Arthur, meows. People think cats don't want to join in, but they're wrong.

Lucille lies in bed, going over everything she'll have to do tomorrow. She's got lists taped to all the kitchen cupboards. She's made the pies and the cranberry sauces and the cupcakes and the whipped cream and the reception salad and the rolls. She made pumpkin tea breads for the guests to take home. Well, the guest. One guest. Maddy's father. She's still not so sure it was a good idea to invite him.

She tries to be a good Christian. Jesus went around forgiving *every*one, though her personal belief is that he went a little too far with that business.

But then she turns over onto her back and thinks about this: there's something she heard once, something about if you can't forgive everything, you can't forgive anything.

Murderers in prison. All those do-gooders who go out and teach them to read and write, and some of those prisoners get a damn good college education, to say nothing of meals and a bed, all courtesy of Lucille and other taxpayers, thank you very much. But murderers in prison. Why did they do it? What led them to do it? Was it in them or *put* in them?

Oh, all right, she'll be gracious. "Welcome!" "Thank you for coming!" "And what do you do for a living?" "Maddy tells me you're quite the fisherman!" and so on and so forth. She'll do it for Maddy, because she loves her. Even though . . .

Lucille turns on the bedside light. Sits up at the side of the bed and tries to calm her roiling feelings. She's worried that if Maddy spends much time with her father, she'll lose confidence in herself. And maybe she's a tiny bit worried that Maddy will go back to him.

Then Lucille sees an envelope slide beneath her door. She fetches it and sits back down to read it. They do this sometimes, slide notes under each other's doors. Maddy finds the most beautiful stationery at the Goodwill and shares it with Lucille. They write notes and give each other stories from the paper or magazines, cartoons, recipes, poems. Sometimes Maddy gives her a crossword puzzle because she's heard such things help aging brains. Well. Sorry, Lucille has no time for such things. You finish and . . . what? You frame it? No. Lucille will stick to her cooking and her arts and crafts. That uses her brain quite enough, thank you.

Lucille opens the envelope. She hopes this is one of those outrageous stories about movie stars embarrassing themselves. She has to admit she likes reading those. Of course, she's not the only one, how do you think those magazines make so much money? She does wish they would bring back periodicals with a bit more class: *Motion Picture. Modern Screen. Photoplay.* Somewhere, pressed in some book, she still has a studio shot of Lana Turner that just takes your breath away. Lucille likes gossip, it's true, but she also used to like the way that movie stars seemed so different from regular people. She didn't agree with something she read in a magazine at the nail parlor Maddy took her to for her birthday—a *pedicure*, Lucille got, which she had always thought of as vain and practically sinful, but oh, my, did it feel good! But anyway, there was a column in the magazine called "Movie Stars! They're Just Like Us!" No, they're not. And we don't want them to be! Just like her, as a teacher. She knows her students want to keep her elevated.

Lucille gets out her glasses and unfolds the paper decorated with two bluebirds. It's a note from Maddy, written in her purple ink, a quote of some kind. Maddy finds the best quotes from all kinds of places, sometimes even from the packs of letters she finds at estate sales. This one says:

What is it that makes a family? Certainly no document does, no legal pronouncement or accident of birth. No, real families come from choices we make about who we want to be bound to, and the ties to such families live in our hearts.

Beneath the quote, Maddy has written, *Thank you for inviting my father, who is not my real family, but to whom I am also tied.*

Lucille presses the note to her bosom. Oh, she loves that girl. She will be the best Thanksgiving hostess ever. Someone should come and film her, they could pick up a lot of good tips. She will be Martha Stewart, or whoever is Martha Stewart these days. She supposes it could be a gay man, that might be a nice change.

She goes back to bed, turns out the light, and can hear herself start to snore before she falls off into sleep. She doesn't know why so many people hate snoring. She finds it soothing. White noise, with a ruffle.

On Thanksgiving Day, Maddy's father arrives ten minutes early. From the living room window, where she and Arthur have just finished building a fire, Maddy sees his car idling at the curb.

"My dad is here!" she says.

Arthur moves to the window and looks out. He knocks, gestures for Steven to come in.

"He can't see you," Maddy says.

"What?"

"He can't see you!"

"Oh." Arthur shuffles slowly toward the coat closet.

"I'll get him," Maddy says. "You'd better go and tell Lucille he's here."

Maddy throws on a jacket and runs outside. Her father sees her before she reaches him, and nods. He turns off the engine and gets out of the car, and his eyes go to her stomach, then to her face. He looks like a man who is stricken, trying not to look stricken. He *is* a man who is stricken, trying not to look that way. He's carrying a wicker basket covered with orange cellophane.

Maddy clasps her hands together. "Come on in!" she calls, shivering.

"Okay," he says, but he doesn't move.

"Dad?"

"Okay," he says, and moves toward her. "You look good," he says, when he reaches her. "It's nice to actually see you in person."

"You, too. Long time." She looks him directly in the eye, and it comes to her that she can't remember ever having done this. She looks him in the eye and she stays even.

"You cold?" he asks.

"I'm fine." She takes his arm and they go inside, where they are greeted by Lucille in her Thanksgiving (cavorting turkeys) apron and by Arthur in his dress slacks and white shirt and blue paisley tie, and by Gordon, who hangs back but lets himself be seen in the little orange-and-brown-checked bow tie Maddy put on him. As for Maddy, she's wearing a brand-new green velvet maternity dress. Her father is in a tan V-neck sweater and brown pants, and Maddy thinks he looks handsome.

"This is for you," Steven says, handing the wicker basket to Lucille.

"Well, *heavens!*" says Lucille. "Will you look at this!" She peers through the cellophane. "Oh, well, Hickory Farms! Who doesn't love that! We will every one of us enjoy this." She smiles at him. "Thank you very much. And welcome!"

"Yes, welcome!" Arthur says. "Would you like a glass of wine? We have red, white, and rosé."

"And sparkling cider," Lucille says. "Also we have some sparkling water."

"And beer," Arthur says.

Maddy has been standing off to the side biting her lip. Now she smiles.

"Well, a glass of red wine would be great," Steven says.

"I'll get it," Maddy says. "You all sit down. You, too, Lucille."

"I have to bring out the appetizers," Lucille says.

"I'll bring them, too."

"Take the *foil* off!" Lucille says, and Maddy says, "Got it."

Arthur and Lucille sit on the sofa and Maddy's father sits in Arthur's recliner. Maddy goes into the kitchen, and from there, she hears Lucille say, "Maddy tells me you're quite the fisherman!"

That night, Maddy sits alone in her room to look at the gift her father brought her. It's a small leather photo album, cracked with age, filled with images of her mother she has never seen before, including one of her pregnant with Maddy. Maddy puts her finger to her mother's belly and holds it there for a while when she comes to that one.

There are photos of her parents' wedding, her mother wearing a simple white dress and baby's breath in her hair, and she and Maddy's father are luminous in their joy. There are photos of the just-marrieds in their Salvation Army apartment, and Maddy looks greedily at everything: not just her mother and her father, but at all the things they had around them. She sees her mother had the same proclivity for funkiness that Maddy does: here is a beautiful shawl over a trunk holding a telephone and an elaborate candelabra. Their bed is a mattress on the floor, and there is a kind of mobile made from hangers over it, crystals and feathers and butterflies made from newspaper all over it. Brick-and-board bookcases full of paperbacks. Coffee-can planters.

There are some photos of Maddy after her mother died, not many and not very good. There's Maddy as a maybe three-month-old (she's guessing, judging from what she's learned), lying on her stomach and looking up like she's confused, a thin line of drool falling from her mouth. There's one of her holding on to the edge of a coffee table— cruising, they call this, the way babies hold on to things before they start walking alone. There's one of her standing beside a body of water, a lake, maybe, and the photo is so blurry she can't really tell how old she was. Three? Four? There's one of her in a little white gown as she graduates kindergarten. One of her in a Brownie uniform, brand-new, and it never got used again, as Maddy didn't feel comfortable in the Brownies, all those little girls so chatty and getting all excited about making God's eyes. She asked to drop out after one meeting, and her father—she still remembers this—said, "Fine, drop out then, don't even try, as usual." There's one of her on her thirteenth birthday shielding her face from the camera. And that's all. There are no more. And there are none of her father and her together. Her father must have had friends at one time, but Maddy cannot remember any. No one came to the house, and Maddy was rarely left with a sitter. Siting with those photos in her lap, Maddy feels for the first time an aching sense of compassion for her father. But also a rush of excitement for what might now finally develop between them.

The mid-December morning sun is pushing so hard through the window it's as though it is knocking. Arthur lies in bed in his blue (ironed!) pajamas, thinking. Life is such a funny thing. It's so funny. So arbitrary-seeming, but sometimes he just can't help but think that there really is a grand plan. In a way, it reminds him of square dancing, how you can see the pattern fully only by looking at it from above, by not being a part of it.

Long time ago, he and Nola used to like to go square dancing. Every Wednesday night, they would put on their outfits and walk over to the high school gymnasium. Arthur wore dress slacks and a kind of Westernized shirt with pearl snap buttons and a bolo tie; Nola wore a white off-shoulder blouse and lots of crinolines beneath a pretty beribboned skirt that would twirl way out and show off her legs. They'd drink punch, eat cookies, and dance the night away.

There was the caller, and he would be standing up on the stage telling everyone what to do. He was like God.

Promenade all, he might say. Start walking through life. *Honor,* he'd call, and the ladies would curtsy and the men would bow, boy, you sure don't see that much anymore. Maybe in England. But yes, *honor:* get married.

When you did the *do-si-do,* why, then your partner would seem to disappear, but she was right behind you. Right there. Like Nola, now. An *angel* was someone who demonstrated the proper movements, well now isn't that true?

Star to the right. Arthur likes to think about that term. Couples walk to each other and join right hands in a star formation and then walk in the direction they are facing. And what he hopes is that he'll see Nola again, and that's how it will be. They'll join hands and walk off together in this new direction they're facing.

But for now he is here, and the birds are singing and Lucille is snoring in the room across the hall and the girl he calls his daughter is frying bacon in the kitchen downstairs and the child he calls his grandchild is stirring in the womb.

Today he'll finish the book he's making for the baby, a proper book of trees. Arthur thinks more people should pay more attention to trees. The names alone! Autumn Splendor buckeye. Regal Prince oak. Shawnee Brave bald cypress. Black tupelo. Skyline honey locust. Happidaze sweet gum. He can't explain it and he wouldn't want anyone to know, but lately when he reads the names of trees, he cries.

When he finishes the book on trees, he'll start one on flowers. Then birds. A lot to do!

He sits up and experiences the kind of dizziness that has

plagued him lately. But then it goes away. Another day! *Promenade all.*

On Chrismas Eve day, Lucille comes in from the front porch, scowling. Maddy, who has just finished cleaning up the needles that were under the Christmas tree, turns off the vacuum and looks over at her.

"What's wrong?"

"Nothing!" Lucille shouts.

Maddy waits.

"It's just that I don't see why he has to go to the cemetery every day, especially when the weather is like this. Look at it out there!"

Maddy looks. It is snowing a little, but nothing to get alarmed about. And it's going up to the forties.

"I worry more about how frail he's become," Maddy says.

"That's what I mean!"

"Well, you said the weather."

"It's all combined!"

Maddy supposes that's true.

"It takes too much *out* of him to go!" Lucille says, and Maddy sits down. There's a rant coming on and she needs to sit down for that. It's a little hard now, standing for long. She feels a certain pressure bearing down all the time. It's from the baby having dropped, her doctor told her. Twice now, she thought she was going into labor, but it was only Braxton-Hicks contractions.

Lucille is going on, in a voice loud enough that Gordon has fled the room. "It would be one thing if he were in shape, but have you listened to his breathing lately? He needs to go to the doctor. I keep telling him he needs to go to the doctor! But he won't go! Oh, isn't it just like a man! He figures he's got two women taking care of him and that's enough. But it's not!

"If we could just get him to stop going to that damn cemetery every day, I'll bet he'd get his strength up. He'd get better. He's going to *kill* himself, going out there. Why does he have to go *out* there?"

"He needs to be with Nola," Maddy says, quietly.

"He's *not* with Nola! She's dead! She was a nice woman, I know he loved her very much, but she is D-E-A-D!"

"I guess not to him," Maddy says.

Lucille looks at her. "Well, fine, I understand that. Frank is not dead to me. But you don't see me traipsing over to his grave to sit over him like some . . . some . . . vulture!"

"That's not fair, Lucille."

She stares at the floor. "I know it's not. I'm sorry I said it. But just because you still love someone is no reason to risk your health the way he's doing. You don't see me running out to Frank's grave in the freezing cold!"

"I thought you said he was cremated."

"Never mind. You know what I mean."

Maddy adjusts the pillow behind her back. Here it comes again, those contractions. Just a big tease.

"I have an idea!" Lucille says. "Why don't we make Arthur a shrine to Nola, right in his room? You know, like those people who make altars and put oranges and beads and candles and whatnot on them? Then he would be with her all the time. If he woke up at night, he could turn on the light, and there she would be. So much easier!"

"He wouldn't go for that," Maddy says.

"Why not?"

Maddy shrugs. "Because she wouldn't be there."

"She's not anywhere!"

Maddy stands and begins pacing. "Well, see, I think that she is there, in the cemetery, for Arthur. Her spirit is strong there. He feels her, and he talks to her. I understand that. I feel things in cemeteries, too, don't you?"

"No. No, I don't and I don't want to. Here is life, and there is death, and that's that. And I'll tell you another thing." Lucille stops talking suddenly and looks at Maddy. "Is that . . . Are you peeing?"

Maddy shakes her head. "It's not pee. I think my water just broke."

"Oh, Lord," Lucille says.

"Call a cab," Maddy says.

"I'll drive, I'll drive, get in the *car!*"

"Call a cab," Maddy says again, firmly. "And leave a note for Arthur."

Rosalind Mathers. Born August 1, 1933. Died August 1, 2011. A scientist of some reputation. Worked in a hospital lab. Married a doctor who worked there. Two blond children who had two blond children.

Timothy "Doc" Stanley. Born June 22, 1950. Died September 4, 2005. An athlete. A sailor, biker, runner, tennis player. And yet. Handsome fellow, yellow hair and green eyes and a Kirk Douglas dimple in his chin. Life of the party, because of his great ability to impersonate anyone. Loved his dogs, always had at least two springer spaniels. Thought it was funny to answer his phone by saying, "You DID?"

Ted Ungeman. Musician. And deaf in one ear!

Arthur coughs. No time for this. He'd better get to Nola.

He hasn't brought his chair today, too hard to carry. He does have half a meatloaf sandwich in one of the pockets of his overcoat, one of Lucille's turtle brownies in the other.

He makes it over to Nola's grave and stands there for a moment, shivering. He supposes he needs a new coat, this one isn't doing the trick anymore. He doesn't have enough fat to keep himself warm, despite Lucille's best efforts. The butter that woman puts on his bread! He ought to buy stock in Land O Lakes!

He takes his sandwich out, unwraps it slowly. "Hello, Nola," he says. "Cold out today. You always did hate the cold. No, don't say any different, I know you did, you just didn't complain about it the way most folks do. As if that would help! Sometimes I wonder what the world would sound like if everybody stopped their complaining. It sure would be a quiet place."

He looks around. A few rows over is a woman standing at the foot of a grave. He gives her a little wave, but he doesn't think she sees him. Her car is parked nearby, the engine still running, and as Arthur watches, she runs over and gets back in and drives away.

He misses driving at times like this. The walk to the stop isn't that long, but the wait for the bus can be.

"Lucille made beef stew last night with a lot of wine in it, and it was really good," Arthur tells Nola. "Remember how we never could understand why people wasted wine by dumping it in food? But it was good! I didn't eat much and she read me the riot act. But I'm just not much hungry anymore." He looks at his half sandwich. "Even this is too much for me. Wish I could share it with you.

"Nola, I wanted to talk to you about something. Remember how we used to worry about who we would leave things to in our will after we were both gone? And we put it off and put it off and we never did make a will. We figured, what difference did it make? That was irresponsible of us. We could have left it to a hospital, or a school, or a cat shelter. Anyway, I had a will made yesterday. You remember Tony Sanders? It's his son, little Jeffrey, who's running the office now, real nice kid, and I had him do it. And I'm leaving everything to that girl. Maddy. I think you'd approve. I know you would. Well, I think I know. Can you give a sign, sweetheart? Anything. Can you just send me a sign?"

Nothing. Not a sound, not a breeze, not a movement of clouds, no birds, no cars, no people. Nothing.

He puts the sandwich back in his pocket and, holding on to Nola's headstone, kneels down and takes off his hat. The earth is so cold. "Nola. I need to tell you something. I can't come out here anymore. It's gotten too hard. I'd like to say I just need some time and then I'll be back again, but I don't think so, sweetheart. I hope you're not disappointed. *I'm* disappointed, but I hope you aren't. I hope you're past all that now, Nola. I hope you're past disappointment and pain and all that. I hope you're just happy, and waiting for me. That's what I hope more than anything in the world." He kisses the headstone, right on the N for Nola Corrine, the Beauty Queen. "I'll love you forever in darkness and sun, I'll love you past when my whole sweet life is done," he says. Something he once wrote to her in a birthday card when they were still in their twenties. Oh, my. In their twenties. And there it is, slow to come today, but there it is, the feeling of her inside him. She blooms in his heart, and he is suddenly warm.

He rises with difficulty, puts his hat back on his head, and walks toward the bus. Once, and only once, he turns back.

Maddy's hospital room looks like a greenhouse. Roses from her father. A wildly colorful mixed bouquet from Mr. Lyons and his wife. A little carnation bouquet with a teddy bear from her new school. And many, many bouquets from Arthur and Lucille.

The cart is loaded up with all her flowers, with all the things the hospital has given her for the baby. Her breasts are leaking, she has dark circles under her eyes, she's wearing a Kotex the size of a barge and a winter coat that has seen its better days, and she has never felt so beautiful in all her life.

The nurse brings her baby in and with exquisite care Maddy turns back a corner of the blanket to look into the sleeping face. She has never felt so beautiful in her life.

Lucille comes into the room and tells her the car is pulled up, they're ready to go. "I have to wait for a wheelchair," Maddy says, and Lucille, alarmed, says, "What happened?"

"Nothing," Maddy says. "That's just the way they do it. You can't walk to the car."

"Oh," Lucille says. She sits on the edge of Maddy's bed. "Well, where *are* they?"

Maddy thinks Lucille, having brought the staff enough cookies to stock a grocery store, expects the royal treatment. And maybe she's getting it, because here comes transportation services already, after she'd been told it would take twenty minutes or so. Maddy sits in the chair and holds the baby close to her, adds another blanket that Lucille crocheted, then another.

It doesn't take long to get home, and when Maddy comes into the house, she climbs the stairs to Arthur's room before she even takes her coat off. He can't get out of bed anymore. He's so beautiful now, he looks like he's made of marble, and his eyes seem always full of light. Lucille can't get him to eat, but she concocted a sort of milkshake that he likes, and Maddy is glad to see his glass is empty.

He's lying still, his eyes closed, and Maddy's heart sinks. But then, "Arthur?" she says, and his eyes pop open.

"Well, look who's here," he says, his voice breaking. And then, "Where's your nose thing?"

Maddy smiles. "I took it out. The baby likes to grab things."

"Oh. Huh. I'd kind of gotten used to it. But you look great without it, too."

He sits up straighter in the bed. "Can I see?"

She lays the baby in his arms, and Arthur looks up at Maddy, who gently holds the baby's waving fist still, lest Arthur get punched in the nose. "This is Truluv," she tells the baby. And then, after Gordon leaves the foot of the bed to come and investigate, she says, "And this is Gordon the cat."

Arthur says something so low Maddy can't quite hear it. "Pardon?"

He is staring wonderstruck into the face of the baby. "I said that now I've had just about everything, haven't I? I've really had just about everything you could ask for in this life."

"And much more to come!"

Arthur nods, unconvincingly. Then he says, "Sit down. Sit down by me, Maddy. I want to tell you something."

Maddy sits on the bed and smiles into his old face with its map of wrinkles and his noble, high cheekbones. She looks at his stick-out ears and his heart beating in his throat.

He says, "Nola once told me she wished people could be stars in the sky and look down on those that they loved. I always wished that could be so. Let's you and I pretend it's true, even if it isn't, would that be okay with you?"

Maddy nods, her throat tight.

"And after I die, why, you look up in the sky for two stars, real close together. That will be Nola and me. Those stars will be so close together, it'll look like they are one, but they'll be two. Me, and then just to my right, Nola. Look up at us sometimes."

"I will," Maddy says, "I promise. But you're not going anywhere yet."

"No, I'm not," Arthur says, looking down at the baby. "We have a lot to discuss. And anyway, I'm feeling a lot better, suddenly."

A beautiful June 1. Beautiful day! Birds twitter in the branches nearby and the graves have been newly tended. Let the visitations begin.

Trudy Billings. Born May 7, 1924. Died October 1, 2016. Predicted when she was sixteen years old that she would die at thirty-five. Made a practice of hysteria but had the good sense to know she was a pain in the ass and in fact requested that "Pain in the ass" be put on her headstone. (Good sense of humor despite her preoccupation with doom and gloom!) Family would not comply with this particular request. So instead what is on her marker is her second choice: FINALLY. Ha ha. She sold clothes at Dacy's until they went out of business. Women's Everyday. Lunch in a sack eaten every day at twelve o'clock in a dressing room. Perfume sprayed onto a cotton ball and stuffed into her brassiere. Liked horror films; she liked to have the bejesus scared out of her. Oh, the dahlias in her garden. Kept her dial phone, which her grandchildren loved.

Patricia Dooley. Born October 29, 1922. Died May 1, 2016. Came from a family of seven girls. An OB nurse, delighted by the birth of every baby, no matter what. A rank sentimentalist. Had one of those plaques in her kitchen that said, "No matter where I serve my guests, it seems they like my kitchen best." Liked the snow. Loved the snow. Made snow angels in every first snowfall until she was ninety.

And now: *Arthur Moses. Born April 3, 1931. Died December 29, 2016.* Maddy's eyes fill. *Mensch. Dear friend. Dearest friend.* She lays a creamy white Full Sail rose on his grave, then bends down to inspect Mr. and Mrs. Hamburger, who are also resting there today. They're fine. Tomorrow they'll move to Nola's grave. For today, Maddy lays a coral-colored Eternal Flame rose there. Maddy brought three roses from Arthur's garden to the cemetery today: one for Arthur, one for Nola, and one for someone else.

She stands and looks out over the acres of land. All the lives. All the whispering she hears! It really is true that cemeteries are busy places. *I lived! I lived! I lived!*

There is a thumping sound and Maddy looks over. "Did you fall down?" she asks.

The toddler nods.

"Are you hurt?"

"No."

"Well, get up," Maddy says, and holds out her arms.

"No!"

Getting into the terrible twos, as people call them, but Maddy doesn't think they're terrible. She thinks two-year-olds are incredibly interesting. And loving. You just need to take the time.

She gets out her camera and takes a few shots. There's a photography exhibit that she's having mounted next week at school. It's called *Old*, and that's what it's about: her appreciation of old people, old things. The prints are done in silver gelatin. The contents of Arthur's kitchen drawer is one of the shots. He and Lucille at the kitchen table, the sun streaming through the window behind them, that's another one. Maybe she'll do a show featuring children next. Other end of the spectrum. She looks at her own child's rumpled brow, the pooched-out lips. The toddler looks like Winston Churchill, deliberating.

Maddy's instructor thinks she will show in New York City someday. And last week she learned that two of her images were bought by *Popular Photography* magazine. Her instructor submitted them without asking her, but she forgives him. She certainly does.

"Nola!" Maddy says. "Get up and come to Mommy." Again she holds out her arms, and now her daughter pushes herself up and runs to her.

When Nola reaches her, Maddy enfolds her in her arms. "Show me a happy girl," she says.

Nola steps away, smiles, then throws back her head and spreads her arms wide.

Maddy laughs. "Should we go now? Want to go and see Grandma Lucille?" Her tenant. And the self-appointed grandmother who is teaching Nola to bake. Already Nola has mastered monkey bread.

They walk hand in hand toward the exit, and Maddy drops the last rose on a stranger's grave, because he is not a stranger at all. It's a Sweet Afton, pearlescent white with a pale pink reverse; she knows its strong scent will last and last. Truluv taught her that.

ACKNOWLEDGMENTS

Many people have gladdened my heart by their warm embrace of *The Story of Arthur Truluv*. Julie Bolton was one of the early readers, and she offered insightful analysis. Kate Medina, my longtime, greatly loved, and highly esteemed editor at Random House, understood this book from the get-go, and told me, "I need an Arthur in my life!" (To which I responded, "Me, too!")

Gina Centrello, thank you so much for your belief in this one.

To vital others on the Random House team—Erica Gonzalez, Anna Pitoniak, Avideh Bashirrad, Paolo Pepe, Joe Perez, Jo Anne Metsch, Leigh Marchant, Andrea DeWerd, Barbara Fillon, Christine Mykityshyn, Beth Pearson, and Susan Brown—please accept my gratitude for your talent and goodwill.

Suzanne Gluck, thank you for your suggestions early on that made the book better. I love that voodoo that you do so well.

To my writing group: Veronica Chapa, Arlene Malinowski, Marja Mills, Pam Todd, and Michele Weldon.

Your honest and enthusiastic response to this material meant everything. Thank you for putting up with my reading such long passages every single week until the thing was done.

Phyllis Florin: You must know how much your words about this book meant to me. But just in case, here it is in black and white.

Last but most, thank you to all the people who read my books and make it possible for me to make a living doing what I love. It still feels like a miracle. May it always.

ABOUT THE AUTHOR

ELIZABETH BERG is the author of many bestselling novels, including *Open House* (an Oprah's Book Club selection), *Talk Before Sleep*, and *The Year of Pleasures*, as well as the short story collection *The Day I Ate Whatever I Wanted*. *Durable Goods* and *Joy School* were selected as ALA Best Books of the Year. She adapted *The Pull of the Moon* into a play that enjoyed sold-out performances in Chicago and Indianapolis. Berg's work has been translated into twenty-seven languages, and three of her novels have been turned into television movies. She is the founder of Writing Matters, a quality reading series dedicated to serving author, audience, and community. She teaches one-day writing workshops and is a popular speaker at venues around the country. Some of her most popular Facebook postings have been collected in *Make Someone Happy*. She lives outside Chicago.

elizabeth-berg.net
Facebook.com/bergbooks

ABOUT THE TYPE

This book was set in Electra, a typeface designed for Linotype by renowned type designer W. A. Dwiggins (1880–1956). Electra is a fluid typeface, avoiding the contrasts of thick and thin strokes that are prevalent in most modern typefaces.